W9-AAP-664

Amy Wall
January 2, 1982
Amy Wall
January 2, 1982
947-8258

THE MYSTERY OF
THE VELVET GOWN

**Trixie
Belden**

Your TRIXIE BELDEN Library

Trixie Belden

MYSTERY OF THE VELVET GOWN

Cover by Ben Otero

BY KATHRYN KENNY

GOLDEN PRESS
Western Publishing Company, Inc.
Racine, Wisconsin

Copyright © 1980 by
Western Publishing Company, Inc.
All rights reserved. Produced in U.S.A.

GOLDEN® , GOLDEN PRESS® , and TRIXIE BELDEN® are
registered trademarks of Western Publishing Company, Inc.

No part of this book may be reproduced or
copied in any form without written permission
from the publisher.

ISBN 0-307-21550-4

All names, characters, and events in this
story are entirely fictitious.

CONTENTS

THE MYSTERY OF
THE VELVET GOWN

The Stage Is Set · 1

FACE FLUSHED and sandy curls tousled in disarray, fourteen-year-old Trixie Belden raced down the south corridor of Sleepyside Junior-Senior High School.

"Hold on there, Miss Belden," a voice boomed. Trixie came to a sudden halt. The clock in science class had ticked away the seconds with painful slowness; every minute had seemed to hold back with selfish disregard, until finally the bell of freedom had rung—and now this!

Trixie turned to find her math teacher, Mr. Sanborn, gazing sternly at her from a classroom doorway, his arms folded on his chest.

"It seems to me, Trixie, that if you were as quick with algebra problems as you are at tearing through the halls between classes, we'd both be a little better off. Now, just where do you think you're going at such a racetrack speed? Is there *really* a fire?"

"Oh, Mr. Sanborn," Trixie cried, relieved to note the twinkle of amusement in his eyes, "the results of the tryouts for *Romeo and Juliet* are being posted right now, and I'm dying to know if—"

"Well, well," Mr. Sanborn reflected, scratching his chin. "In the name of the arts and William Shakespeare—and in order to spare you an untimely death—I'll let you go this time. But let's try to keep it to a slow jog."

"Yes, sir. Thank you, Mr. Sanborn," Trixie said quickly, before he had a chance to say something else about her math ability—or inability. At a slightly slower pace, she headed for the drama club office at the end of the long corridor.

The freshman class play was an annual event at Sleepyside High. On the first day of school after the Christmas holidays, tryouts were held.

Every freshman took part in some way, as a member of either the cast or the crew. Experienced juniors and seniors acted as aides, giving help to the freshmen on lighting sets, makeup, stage direction, and costumes.

Trixie had already signed up as a stagehand. Her best friend, Honey Wheeler, was an excellent seamstress and was on the costume crew. The most exciting thing was that their good friend Diana Lynch had actually tried out for the part of Juliet. Di had spent weeks working on her speaking voice, projection, and poise, and on learning her lines. It had taken a lot of prompting from both Honey and Trixie to get Di to go through with the tryout, for she was shyer than either of her friends.

As Trixie hurried down the hallway, she thought, *Di is so pretty,* with *her shiny black hair and violet-colored eyes, she'd make a perfect Juliet. She's just* got *to get the part!*

Trixie was so preoccupied with thoughts of the play and of Di as Juliet that she forgot to watch where she was going, and she collided with someone in front of her.

"Oh, excuse me!" she cried as books fell to the floor and papers flew in all directions.

"Well, Miss Bulldozer!"

"Oh, it's only you," Trixie sighed, realizing that the victim was her brother Mart.

"*Only* me! Only your ever-diligent, always supportive big brother! What's with you, fuzz-brain, running into innocent bystanders like that? Especially when *I* happen to be the innocent bystander!"

"Oh, Mart, my mind was on the play and Di and—"

"And if you ever concentrated on one thing at a time," Mart interrupted, "even something as elementary as getting yourself from one place to another—"

"Mart, puh-leeze don't start that. All I wanted to do was find out if Di got the part or not."

"Relax, Trixie," Mart said, helping her retrieve her books and papers. "The notice hasn't been posted yet. But somewhere in that mob over there," he continued, motioning toward the large group crowded around the drama club office, "I'm sure you'll find our aspiring thespian friend."

Just then, Honey joined them. She was taller and slimmer than Trixie, and she had hazel eyes. Her shoulder-length, golden-brown hair and her sweet disposition had earned her the nickname of Honey.

"I tried to get here sooner," Honey gasped, trying to catch her breath, "but I had to help wash petri dishes in biology lab, and then I dropped one and it broke and I had to clean it up, and you know how I hate that slimy stuff—"

"Hold it, hold it!" Mart cried. "First I act as a set of brakes for Trixie, and then I have to hear a thirty-three rpm record playing at seventy-eight. Calm down, Honey. There's no news yet."

As he spoke, a small woman with short, curly dark hair and bright green eyes emerged from the drama club office.

Trixie whispered to Mart, "That's the new drama teacher, Miss Darcy." Mart nodded but didn't turn his head. *Why, he's as excited as I am*, Trixie thought.

"Boys and girls," Miss Darcy was saying, "I know you are all very anxious to hear the results of the tryouts, so instead of posting them and having you all fight for a view, I shall read the list." She glanced down at the paper in her hand. "Tybalt will be played by Paul Victors,

Mercutio by John Munter, Romeo by Jamie
Kenworthy, and Juliet by Diana Lynch. All
other parts, including the chorus and atten-
dants, will be posted. The play will open on
Valentine's Day, February fourteenth, so we
have lots of work to do in the next six weeks.
Drama class and rehearsals begin tomorrow.
Congratulations, everyone."

The hush that had descended over the group
while Miss Darcy was speaking was broken as a
wave of cheers and shouts swept through the
crowd. Trixie, Honey, and Mart spotted Di,
looking somewhat dazed as other classmates offered her their congratulations.

"I *knew* you'd get the part, Di. I just *knew* it!"
Trixie cried, giving Di a quick hug.

"You'll be wonderful," Honey added warmly.

"Imagine—a Shakespearean heroine in our
midst. Congratulations, fair Juliet!" Mart exclaimed, falling to one knee.

Di giggled nervously. "I still can't believe
it—" she began, but the sudden jangling of a
bell interrupted her.

"Jeepers!" cried Trixie. "I don't have my
math book, and I've got algebra this hour, and
now I'm late for class, and—oh, Mr. Sanborn is

sure to have my head this time!''

"Frankly, Beatrix," Mart snickered, "I don't know what he'd do with such a totally useless container."

"Oooh, Mart Belden, I'll. . . ." Trixie shouted over her shoulder as she ran down the hallway. She could hear Mart laughing behind her, but she didn't have time for revenge now; she'd get back at him later. In addition, she *hated* to be called *Beatrix!*

Trixie managed to slide into her seat just as Mr. Sanborn arrived. She was called on to do the first problem, but fortunately, Brian had helped her with all those x and xy equations the night before, and she had the answer. After that, though, her thoughts quickly drifted away from the classroom. Algebra was certainly mysterious, but it was not the kind of mystery that Trixie most liked to tackle.

Trixie seldom questioned her seemingly uncanny ability to attract mysteries wherever she went. She and Honey had solved a number of baffling cases together, and they were determined that one day they would have their own detective agency.

Trixie began to relive some of their past

adventures. *I wonder how Uncle Andrew is doing*, she thought, recalling the time that she and her friends had visited the Iowa sheep farm that belonged to her father's brother. She shuddered slightly as she remembered how she, Honey, and Jim had been stranded on top of an old barn while floodwaters rushed and swirled ominously below them. They had climbed higher and higher as the threatening waters rose, until finally, Mart had come to their rescue. *Of course*, Trixie thought to herself, *we did solve the mystery of Uncle Andrew's missing sheep, which made it all worthwhile.*

That memory triggered another and then still more as Trixie slipped deeper into her daydreaming. She had just begun doodling BELDEN-WHEELER DETECTIVE AGENCY on her notebook, when the sound of Mr. Sanborn's voice snapped her back to the reality of the classroom.

"Trixie?" he questioned sternly. "Are you with us, or are you contemplating the achievements of Euclid?"

"I—I—" Trixie began, but miraculously the bell rang. "Saved again," she mumbled under her breath, and not daring even to glance at Mr. Sanborn, she gathered up her books and quickly left the classroom. She then went to study hall, since drama class was not meeting that day.

Tonight I'm really going to study, she thought as she headed for her locker following study hall. *How am I going to be a great detective and solve mysteries if I can't even solve these awful algebra problems?*

Trixie opened her locker and was met with an avalanche of books and papers. *"Oh, no!"* she groaned, bending down to pick up the mess. *If Moms saw this*, Trixie thought guiltily, *she'd never forgive me. I guess I need to get a little more organized—but not now.* She grabbed her lunch, threw everything else back into the locker, and quickly slammed the door before the assemblage of junk had a chance to counter-attack. "I'll leave lunch early and clean it up," she said firmly as she headed for the cafeteria to meet her friends.

Honey, Di, and Mart were already there when Trixie arrived.

"Well, Trixie," Mart teased, "I see you haven't been decapitated, after all. You probably conned Mr. Sanborn with some quick answers, courtesy of our benevolent older brother."

"Why don't you spend lunch hour in the library, Mart—eating dictionaries?" Trixie retorted, not yet ready to forgive him for having called her by her hated full name. Besides, Mart's constant use of big words irritated her.

"Where *is* that famous older brother of yours? And where's *my* brother?" Honey asked quickly, well aware that arguments between Mart and Trixie could sometimes get out of hand. "I'm sure Di is anxious to tell them about the play."

"I believe," Mart answered, "that they were recently in the pursuit of physical adeptness and skill in aquatic sports, and they are undoubtedly waiting to cleanse themselves of chlorinated H two O."

"You mean they just had swimming class and probably got held up in the line for showers," Honey interpreted.

"Exactly," Mart said, smiling.

Just then, the duo joined them at the table. Brian Belden, Trixie and Mart's older brother, was tall and good-looking, with dark, wavy hair. He was often told that he was an exact duplicate of his father, while fair-haired, blue-eyed Mart, Trixie, and six-year-old Bobby, the youngest Belden, resembled their mother.

Jim Frayne was Honey's adopted brother. He'd had a hard life with a cruel stepfather who mistreated him. He had finally run away, and primarily through Trixie and Honey's efforts, he had been adopted by Honey's parents. He had a quick temper, which Trixie attributed to his red hair, but he also had a quick smile and a generous nature. He hoped to open a school for boys one day, with the money he had inherited from his great-uncle, a wealthy old miser who had lived near the Belden home. Jim had come to Sleepyside to find his great-uncle after running away from his stepfather, but the old man had died before Jim ever reached him.

The two boys sat down at the table, and Trixie began excitedly, "Brian, Jim, you'll never guess what happened to—"

"Trixie," Honey interrupted, "maybe Di would like to tell her own news."

"Gleeps!" Trixie cried, putting her hand over her mouth. "You're right. Sometimes I think I only open my mouth to change feet. I'm sorry, Di. You tell them."

"Well," Di began, blushing slightly, "I got the part of Juliet in the freshman class play. . . ."

Her voice trailed off uncertainly.

"Congratulations!" Brian and Jim said in unison.

"But what's wrong, Di?" Brian asked. "You're not exactly acting like you're on cloud nine—or even cloud eight-and-a-half."

"Oh, no," Di answered quickly. "I'm really *very* excited and honored. It's just that now that I have the part, I'm not sure I'll be able to do it."

"Opening night jitters before rehearsals have started!" Jim exclaimed. "Don't worry, Di. We'll all help you learn your lines, if that's what you're worried about. You'll be great."

"I hope so," Di sighed. "It's just that I feel like a hundred butterflies have been let loose in my stomach."

"*Lepidoptera* could not possibly survive the intestinal secretions of the digestive cavity," Mart spouted.

"And one *Trixieda*," said Trixie, "cannot possibly survive the pain in the digestive tract one brother gives *her*."

"Ah, *little* sister," Mart began, with emphasis on the word "little." People often mistook them for twins because they looked so much alike.

Mart was always careful to explain that he was a full eleven months older than Trixie. If she hated being called Beatrix, the thing he hated the most was for people to think that they were twins.

"Peace, siblings, peace," Brian laughed. "No one will be able to keep anything in his or her digestive tract with you two causing such an uproar. Besides, I want to hear more about the play."

"Well, okay," Trixie began. "I'm going to be a stagehand and Honey's on the costume crew."

"It's lucky that it's not the other way around," Brian teased, "knowing *your* dexterity with a needle."

"Are you kidding?" Trixie laughed good-naturedly. "Me on a costume crew? They don't need Halloween costumes, Brian. This is Shakespeare! But Honey will be great," she continued. "She did such a terrific job on our club jackets."

The "club" was the Bob-Whites of the Glen, or B.W.G.'s, for short. It was a semisecret club formed to help people in need. The members included all those at the lunch table, plus Dan Mangan, the most recent member of the group.

Dan, whose goal was to become a policeman, had been brought to Sleepyside by his uncle, Bill Regan, the Wheelers' groom. Having once been in trouble as a member of a tough New York City street gang, Dan was now interested in finding solutions to the problem of juvenile crime. He had received special permission from his school counselor to attend a two-week seminar in New York City on neighborhood youth programs.

"It will be great working with Miss Darcy. She's a terrific drama teacher," Di said.

"And Miss Trask is so glad to have her here," Honey said.

Honey's parents were wealthy, and she had always had a governess. Miss Trask had been her governess for a while, but now that Honey was old enough, she no longer needed one. Miss Trask had stayed on with the Wheelers, however, to manage their huge estate.

"Isn't Miss Trask a friend of Miss Darcy's mother?" Trixie asked.

"Yes," Honey answered. "Her mother died when Miss Darcy was a little girl, and then she and her father moved to London. He's an assistant to an ambassador there. Miss Trask hadn't seen Miss Darcy in years, and then Miss Darcy came to New York for a visit, and she just decided to stay. Teaching jobs are very difficult to find in London, and when one opened up right here—well, it was just too good to pass up!"

"You know what else is nice?" Trixie added. "We've never been able to participate in extracurricular activities, living so far from town. But with rehearsals during drama class and the second half of lunch hour, we can do it."

"Extra curricular!" Jim hooted. "You've been enough 'extracurricular activity' for every high school in New York State ever since I met you, Trixie. Wherever you go, you always get us into something. The B.W.G.'s have always had a one-person activity department."

Trixie sniffed, pretending to be offended. "I'm not quite sure how to take that."

"The right way," Jim said, smiling. "It's a compliment."

Trixie smiled, too, as she got up from the table. "Right now I have a little extracurricular activity of my own, called 'Locker Clean-Up,' or I might get a concussion the next time I try to open it when I'm in a hurry."

"Which is about ninety-nine percent of the time," Mart laughed.

Trixie excused herself from the table, while the others stayed on to talk before their next classes.

The halls were empty when Trixie returned to her locker. She dialed the lock combination and opened the door. Much to her relief, everything stayed in place. She quickly began pulling out gym equipment, textbooks, notebooks, and other odds and ends, attempting to give the whole mess some semblance of order. She was working busily, when suddenly she became aware of voices nearby.

"I don't know *how* Di Lynch got that part."

"Now, Jane, everyone can't have the lead. Besides, you're on costume crew."

"So what? I should be playing Juliet. I took drama lessons all through elementary school," the one called Jane replied. "That whole gang makes me sick, Patty. Honey's so rich, and Trixie thinks she's such a smart detective. *I* think she's just plain *nosy.*"

"That's not fair, Jane. She's done a lot of good. Remember, she got Hoppy back for the town hall."

Trixie froze. She wasn't sure whether or not
to step out from behind the concealment of her
locker door, but she decided to stay put. When
she heard the two girls turn and go down the
side corridor, Trixie strained to hear the rest of
their conversation.

"I suppose that's true," she heard Jane say,
"but the police could have done the same thing,
and that's *their* job, not Trixie Belden's."

Tears stung Trixie's eyes. She recognized the
voices as those of Jane Morgan and Patty Morris, two classmates. She had never imagined
that anyone felt that way.

Then suddenly, her hurt turned to anger as
Jane concluded, "Whatever the case, Patty, I'm
going to make Diana Lynch sorry she ever tried
out for the part of Juliet."

The Accident • 2

EVEN THOUGH Trixie had a busy afternoon of classes, Jane Morgan's comments kept bothering her, like an itch that wouldn't go away. Lost in thought, Trixie was strangely quiet as she joined the other Bob-Whites on the school bus.

"What's the matter, Trixie?" Honey asked, noticing her friend's unusual silence.

"I was just thinking."

"Uh-oh," Mart interjected. "That's when it's time for *us* to start worrying. Remember, Trixie, *Romeo and Juliet* is not a mystery; it's a tragedy."

"I know." Mart glanced at her sharply. It wasn't like Trixie to ignore his teasing. "I was just wondering," she said, turning to Honey and Di. "Do you know Jane Morgan?"

"I went to elementary school with her when we lived in town," Di answered, "and she's in a few of my classes now. But I don't know her very well."

"Neither do I," Honey echoed. "I've probably spoken fewer than ten words to her in my entire life. Why do you ask?"

"No reason." Trixie shrugged, deciding that Jane's comments would only hurt Di's feelings and that it was probably just jealousy on Jane's part, anyway. *For once*, Trixie thought, giving herself a mental pat on the back, *I thought before I spoke.*

It was snowing lightly when they left school, but as the bus turned onto Glen Road and headed east, the wind picked up and sent snowflakes swirling in a crazy dance.

Trixie pressed her nose against the bus window. "Wouldn't it be *awful*," she giggled, "if it snowed all night and we couldn't go to school tomorrow?"

"It certainly would," Honey agreed. "We'd

31

have a whole day to do all those boring things like sledding and having snowball fights."

Brian sighed with mock sympathy. "But Trixie would miss her favorite class—algebra!"

"Terrible, just terrible," Jim laughed.

The school bus pulled up at the end of the driveway at Crabapple Farm and deposited Honey and Jim and the three Beldens. Brian walked directly up the drive, and Honey and Jim turned off onto the path up to Manor House. But Mart and Trixie walked slowly, taking in the quiet beauty of the snow.

There was a blanket of snow on the roof and on the lawn, framing the house with still whiteness. Ice clung to the dark, bare branches of trees and bushes in delicate, lacy patterns. Icicles hung from the eaves of the roof in stark, sculptured beauty. The two Beldens stood in silence for several minutes, then slowly walked up the drive together.

They were greeted at the back door by six-year-old Bobby, who held a freshly baked cookie in each hand.

"Hi, Mart. Hi, Trixie. Wanna oatmeal cookie?" the little boy shouted. He handed them each a warm cookie, then raced back to the table to get one for himself.

"Mmmmmm," Mart sighed, taking a big bite of the hot, spicy cookie, "my favorite."

"Funny how anything edible seems to be your favorite," Trixie teased.

"It's just that cold weather happens to increase my appetite," Mart replied with mock defensiveness.

"Uh-huh," Trixie said, "along with rainy weather, hot weather, partly cloudy weather—and whether or not you've just had a six-course dinner."

"I knew it was too quiet around here," Helen Belden laughed, greeting each of her "twins" with a kiss on the cheek.

"Trixie!" Bobby interrupted. "Moms said you'd help me build a snowball man. Please, Trixie, will you, right now?"

"Now, Bobby, I said you should wait to *ask* Trixie. At least let her get in the door and change out of her school clothes."

Trixie bent down and gave Bobby a hug. Even though he was a bother sometimes and seemed to have an endless supply of questions, she loved him dearly.

"Moms is right, Bobby. Let me change my clothes and have some more of those yummy cookies, and then we'll go out and make a 'snowball man' and angels."

"Angels?" He frowned in puzzlement.

"Snow angels, honey. I'll show you."

"Speaking of angels," Mrs. Belden said, "it's already the third of January, and we still don't have the Christmas tree down. I keep hearing promises from all of you that you'll help pack ornaments. Well, tonight's the night, gang. Don't make any plans for after dinner."

"I'll help," Brian said, "and I'm sure Mart will offer his services, too, as soon as he swallows those three cookies he just put in his mouth."

Mart gave his brother one of his famous why-does-this-always-happen-to-me looks, but he nodded agreement.

"I putted in the raisings all by myself and stirred and stirred till my arm hurted," Bobby said proudly. "And then I let Reddy lick the spoon."

"You *what?*" Mrs. Belden cried as Mart choked on a mouthful of cookies.

"But I didn't put it back in the bowl," Bobby

answered quickly, sensing that he had said the wrong thing.

At the sound of his name, Reddy, the Beldens' big Irish setter, came running into the kitchen. Untrained and totally unpredictable, Reddy was hopeless as a hunter or a watchdog, but all the Beldens loved him, especially Bobby.

"Can Reddy play snow angel, too?" Bobby asked.

"I don't think he'll be able to, Bobby, but he can come out and play snow doggy," Trixie replied. "You start getting into your snowsuit while I go up and change."

"Okey-dokey, Trixie," Bobby said, already struggling into bulky snow pants.

Outside, Trixie taught Bobby how to sit down carefully in the snow and then lie back and move his arms up and down to make a snow angel.

"Yours looks better than mine, Trixie. Mine gets crooked from my elbow," Bobby complained.

"You'll get better at it," she reassured him. "Just keep practicing." They continued playing happily until their mother called them in for dinner.

Peter Belden had just come in from work. He

was a bank officer with the First National Bank of Sleepyside. Trixie and Bobby greeted him with cold, snowy kisses.

Dinner was accompanied by discussions of the freshman class play, the prospect of another heavy snowfall, and, of course, Bobby's account of making snow angels. Just as they were finishing dessert, the telephone rang.

"I'll get it," Mart said, getting up quickly. "It's for you, Trixie," he yelled. "It's Di."

He returned to the dining room. "I swear she must send up smoke signals to her friends, instructing them to call just when she's supposed to start the dishes," he grumbled.

"Now, Mart," Mrs. Belden said. "She played with Bobby for quite a long time after school while you had time to yourself. I think you and Brian could do the dishes this evening and give Trixie some time to *her*self."

Mart grumbled again, but he knew his mother was right. Trixie smiled appreciatively at her mother as she went to answer the phone.

"Hi, Di," Trixie said enthusiastically. "How does your family feel about having a Juliet in their midst?"

"Mummy and Daddy think it's wonderful!"

Di answered. "So wonderful, in fact, that they want me to have a cast party after the last performance. Won't that be terrific?"

Trixie agreed that it would be, and for the next fifteen minutes, they discussed plans for the party. "I'm going to call Honey and tell her," Di finally said. "See you tomorrow on the bus."

Trixie hung up the phone and went to help Mart and Brian put the finishing touches on the washing of the dinner dishes.

"Perfect timing, as usual," Brian laughed, drying the last plate.

Remembering their promise to help untrim the Christmas tree, they all went upstairs to the attic and brought down the empty ornament boxes. They were wrapping the delicate glass pieces in tissue when the back doorbell rang.

"I'll get it," Mr. Belden said. He went through the swinging door to the kitchen and returned a moment later. "There is a Miss Wheeler here to see you, Trixie," he announced formally. "However, she is cleverly disguised as the abominable snowman."

Trixie went out to the kitchen to greet her guest and found her struggling to remove her boots. A heavy layer of snow clung to Honey's hat and coat. Even her eyelashes were iced with a thin layer of snowflakes.

"My goodness!" Trixie cried. "I thought it had stopped snowing. I'm always glad to see you, Honey, but why did you come out in this weather?"

"I've got something *terribly* important to tell you," Honey began. "I tried to call you," she continued, removing her hat and gloves, "but your line was busy. Then I tried to call Di, but her line was busy, too, so I figured you were talking to each other and I didn't know how long you would talk. Mother and Daddy went into New York City this afternoon and won't be back tonight, and Jim had a biology report to do. So Miss Trask said I could walk over to see you, because I wanted someone to talk to, but it wasn't snowing so hard when I left, and you know how I like to walk in the snow, and. . . ."

"Honey, slow down!" Trixie cried. "I know I'm just as bad as you are at getting information out sometimes, but what's *wrong?*"

"Oh, the most awful thing has happened. I just—" By this time, Honey had removed all her snowy outdoor gear, and she and Trixie went into the Beldens' living room. Everyone greeted Honey warmly, particularly Bobby, who loved to have her visit.

"How nice to see you, Honey," Mrs. Belden said. "Please sit down and make yourself at home. We'll soon be done with the tree."

"I'll help, too," Honey said.

Meanwhile, Trixie had been making wild and exasperated gestures, trying to get Honey's attention. "Honey Wheeler," she finally demanded. "Will you please stop being polite for five seconds and tell me what this 'terribly important' thing is that brought you over here tonight?"

"Oh," said Honey, somewhat startled. "That's right." Then her tone became serious as she told her news. "You'll never believe it, Trixie, but Miss Darcy's father is missing—and Scotland Yard suspects that he's been kidnapped!"

"That's terrible!" Helen Belden cried.

"Uh-oh," Mart warned. "Better watch out, or we'll all be at Kennedy International waving good-bye to Trixie on her way to give Scotland Yard a helping hand."

"Cut it out, Mart," Trixie said seriously. "This is nothing to joke about." She turned back to Honey. "Do you know any more details?" she asked.

"Not really," Honey replied. "Miss Trask said that Miss Darcy was too upset to talk very much when she called. All I know is that Miss Darcy received a phone call from the British Embassy in Washington, D.C., when she returned from school late this afternoon. Her father has been missing for a week, but they'd been postponing contacting her, in the hope that they would find him quickly."

"Did they check with all the hospitals and with any other relatives?" Trixie asked, her detective's instincts searching out possibilities and explanations. "Has anyone received a ransom note?"

"Scotland Yard isn't exactly a small-time operation, Trixie," Brian said. "I'm sure they're doing what needs to be done."

"That poor young woman," Mrs. Belden sighed. "She must feel so helpless, being so far away."

"Miss Trask told Miss Darcy she'd come and stay with her or she could come and spend the night at our house, but Miss Darcy insisted that she'd be all right," Honey said as she helped remove ornaments from the tree.

Trixie began to help again, too. The discussion of the kidnapping continued, with Honey repeating all the information she knew.

"I don't mean to change the subject," Honey interjected, "but this ornament is beautiful." She held up a delicately painted lamb.

"That was my grandmother's," Helen Belden said. "Be very careful wrapping it. So many of these ornaments have special meanings," she went on. "Most of them have been passed from generation to generation, like family heirlooms."

"Ah, yes," Mart rhapsodized, holding up a lopsided styrofoam square decorated with a hodgepodge of felt and sequins. "Note the aesthetic excellence of this lovely legacy."

"That was Trixie's first-grade Christmas project." Mrs. Belden smiled. "It is lovely, isn't it?" No one else shared her enthusiasm, and Mart snorted, but Bobby was fascinated.

"Trixie was in first grade?" he asked with amazement. "Just like me?"

"Just like you," Trixie answered. "Brian and Mart were in the first grade at one time, too. In fact, here's *Mart's* first-grade Christmas project." She giggled, displaying a strange-looking star, covered with glitter and bits of cotton. "It's just about as 'lovely' as mine!"

Finally, all the ornaments were packed and ready to be put away in the attic until the next Christmas. Brian, Mart, and Mr. Belden took the tree out of its stand and carried it outside to be chopped up for firewood. Honey and Trixie sat down in front of the fire, while Mrs. Belden and Bobby went to the kitchen to make hot chocolate.

"Trixie," Honey whispered when everyone had left the room, "I have one more thing I've been saving to tell you, but it's a secret, and you have to *promise* not to tell a soul."

"You know I can keep a secret," Trixie said.

"I know you can, Trixie, but I just had to say that, because if Miss Trask ever knew that you knew, she'd know that I was the only other one who knew who could have told you, and you know—Oh, my goodness! *I* don't even know what I'm saying anymore!"

Trixie laughed and nodded understandingly. Both she and Honey had the same tendency sometimes to let their words trip over each other in a mad scramble to get from ideas to sentence forms.

"We're just lucky we can understand each other's gibberish," Trixie giggled. "And I *do* know what you're talking about, even though I still don't know what you want me to pretend I don't know."

"Please, don't *you* start, Trixie," Honey laughed. "I'll tell you right away and spare us both any more fumbling. Do you know that man who often picks up Miss Darcy after school?"

"Sure," Trixie answered. "The one who looks like a cross between Robert Redford and Paul Newman—who could miss him?"

"His name is Peter Ashbury, and Miss Darcy is engaged to him," Honey said excitedly. "Miss Trask was planning to give an engagement dinner for them next week, and as a surprise, she was going to ask Miss Darcy's father to come over from London. Of course, that's all changed now. I just hope they find her father soon!"

"So do I," Trixie sighed, "and I sure wish we could be there to help. Oh," she said suddenly. "With all the talk about the kidnapping, I almost forgot to tell you about Jane Morgan!"

"Jane?" Honey asked. "That's the second

time you've brought her up today. Why are you suddenly so interested in her?"

"I'm not," Trixie explained, "but for some reason, she's interested in us, or at least in Di." Trixie related the conversation she had overheard between Jane Morgan and Patty Morris.

"That's terrible!" Honey exclaimed with wide-eyed disbelief. "I can't imagine anyone being that jealous of us. I mean, I feel so lucky to have friends like you and your brothers and Di and Dan and a brother like Jim—I never even thought about anyone being jealous!"

"I think it's mainly Di getting the part of Juliet that's brought out the green-eyed monster in Jane," Trixie said. "But I do think we should keep an eye on her. Di has enough on her mind with that part right now. She doesn't need any trouble from Jane Morgan."

Honey nodded to show that she understood. Then she glanced down at her watch. "Heavens!" she cried. "Miss Trask will kill me for staying so long. Once I start talking to you and your family, Trixie, you practically have to put a plug in my mouth to get me to stop."

"That isn't how you used to be. Once you were all ribbons and lace and *so* quiet," Trixie teased, recalling the painfully shy Honey Wheeler she had met not all that long ago. Honey had lived at boarding schools and summer camps most of her life, until her father bought the huge old estate near Sleepyside. It was the first time Honey had ever had a real home and a friend like Trixie.

"Oh, golly! I was even terrified of my own shadow!" Honey laughed good-naturedly. "I certainly like myself much better now, without all that ribbon and lace," she added, looking down at her faded dungarees and loose sweater. "And I don't think anyone I know would use the word 'quiet' to describe me anymore!"

"That's for sure," Mrs. Belden agreed as she walked into the room, carrying a tray laden with cups of steaming-hot chocolate.

"Moms," Trixie asked, "could Brian and Mart and I walk Honey home?"

Mrs. Belden agreed but insisted that they all have a cup of hot chocolate before they left.

Soon they were all bundled up for the crisp night air. Bobby pleaded to go, too, but was told it was too late for him. He pouted as he waved good-bye to Honey.

Outside, they had a quick snowball fight,

45

which Mart instigated by hitting Trixie square- ly on the back with a well-packed ball. That sent all of them scrambling, packing, and throwing, until finally they called a truce. But Mart had run on ahead, and Trixie suspected he was stockpiling snowballs for an ambush.

"Shhhh. We'll sneak up on *him* instead," she whispered to Brian and Honey.

Stealthily, they crept forward in the quiet night. The silence was suddenly, sickeningly broken by the screech of tires and the thud of an impact—followed by a child's high, piercing scream.

"That's Bobby!" Trixie cried.

To the Rescue • 3

TRIXIE, HONEY, AND BRIAN raced through the snow, following the sound of Bobby's screams. Mart was close behind them. Up ahead, they could see a car, its rear wheels sunken deep in the snow-filled ditch beside the road. The beams of its headlights cut through the dark night at a crazy angle.

They arrived at Glen Road to find Eileen Darcy bent over Reddy, who was lying in the snow, trembling and whimpering softly.

Bobby was sobbing hysterically. "I w-w-wanted to c-c-come with you, Trixie! An'—an' so did

R-R-Reddy! An' now he's d-d-dead!''

Trixie knelt down and wrapped her arms around the terrified little boy. "Hush, Bobby. It's okay. Reddy's okay," she crooned, looking questioningly at Brian.

Brian was examining the Irish setter's front leg, which was bent and bloody.

"I think it's just a broken leg," he said, "but we'd better get him to the vet right away."

Brian removed his coat and gently wrapped it around the shaking dog. "He's in shock," Brian explained. "We've got to keep him warm. Trixie, you get in the backseat and guide him in. Mart, help me pick him up. Then you and Honey take Bobby home. Trixie will come to the vet's with me."

Quickly, efficiently, everyone did as they were told. Miss Darcy stood there helplessly, wringing her hands and crying, "I didn't even see him. I'm so sorry. I can't. . . ."

"Please, Miss Darcy," Brian said firmly. "I think he's going to be all right. Do you think you could drive us? If not, I could drive."

Honey, often queasy at the sight of blood, held Bobby, trying to soothe him and quiet his cries: "He's dead, and it's my fault!"

"He's not dead, Bobby. Brian's here now, and he's going to take him to the doctor. Everything will be all right." But Honey's voice was shaky and unsure.

Eileen Darcy handed Brian the car keys. He started the engine, carefully pulled the old car forward onto Glen Road, and headed east toward town and the veterinarian's.

In the backseat, Trixie held Reddy's head gently in her lap, stroking him and softly whispering words of reassurance. But her heart was beating rapidly, and she kept thinking, *Please, Reddy, you've got to be all right!*

Brian gripped the wheel firmly and drove in silence. Eileen Darcy, who had been frantically apologizing, was now strangely quiet. Finally, Trixie broke the silence.

"What happened, Miss Darcy?" she asked quietly.

There was a rush of words, as if the woman had been waiting for someone to confront her with the question. "Oh, Trixie, Brian, I'm so sorry! I—I was driving out to see Miss Trask. My father—"

"We heard about your father," Trixie interrupted gently, "and we're sorry."

Eileen Darcy went on, speaking rapidly. "I felt so helpless being in my rooms alone, and Miss Trask had offered to let me spend the night with her. Then, when I got the letter, I—"

"What letter?" Trixie asked.

"From—from a friend in England. She had seen my father recently, and she wrote that he was in good spirits, but that he missed me. And now—oh, I should never have left home!" she cried and buried her face in her hands.

After several minutes, she cleared her throat and began again. "I suppose I should not have even attempted to drive out here tonight, but the snow had stopped, and the driving was quite all right. I'd just realized that I'd missed the turn for Manor House, when suddenly I hit an icy patch in the road, and your dog ran toward the car. I didn't see him until it was too late. I tried to swerve and miss him, but. . . . I'm so sorry." Her voice was shaking as she turned and spoke to Trixie. "How is he?"

"He seems to have stopped trembling so much," Trixie answered, "but his breathing is very heavy. It'll be okay, Reddy," she whispered to the Irish setter, stroking his silky fur. "We're almost there."

Brian finally spoke. "I really do think it's only a broken leg, but we'll soon know."

"It's a good thing you were there, Brian," Trixie said. "He plans to be a doctor," she added to Miss Darcy.

"Here we are," Brian said, pulling into Dr. Samet's driveway.

The old veterinarian had lived in the same large, white clapboard house for as long as Trixie could remember. He not only tended sick family pets, but also cattle, horses, and other large animals in the area. The first floor of his house was devoted to his practice, and he lived on the second floor. An additional room in the back of the house served as a shelter for stray animals that the doctor was always trying to find homes for.

As soon as the car had stopped, Eileen Darcy jumped out and ran up the front steps of the doctor's house to ring the bell. Trixie and Brian slowly and carefully maneuvered Reddy out of the backseat of the car.

Miss Darcy pressed the bell again and again, until finally lights came on inside the house. The door was opened by the doctor, who was dressed in pajamas and a robe. His dark gray

51

hair was rumpled, and he looked as if he had been awakened from a deep sleep.

"Yes?" he asked, not recognizing the young teacher.

"We've brought a dog. I—I hit him accidentally," Miss Darcy stammered as Trixie and Brian carefully carried Reddy up the front steps.

"Trixie! Brian!" Dr. Samet exclaimed. "And Reddy, isn't it? Bring him in, bring him in." The doctor opened the door wider and motioned them toward one of the examining rooms.

Trixie and Brian laid Reddy gently on the clean white table. Dr. Samet spoke soothing words to the frightened dog as he began examining his leg.

"Hold him still, Brian," Dr. Samet instructed, "while I clean this leg. Trixie, you pet him and keep talking to him. This is going to hurt him a bit."

The doctor worked quietly for a while. Finally he said, "It's a pretty bad break—two breaks, actually, but they're confined to this bone. No damage to his rib cage, which is good. He'll have to be in a cast for several weeks. I'd like to keep him here for a few days to watch him and to make sure that he stays off this leg. I remember he was a pretty frisky pup. I'll set his leg and then give him something to help him sleep. He'll be fine. Don't worry."

Tears filled Trixie's eyes, and she bent down and gently hugged Reddy. "Oh, Reddy," she murmured.

Eileen Darcy and Brian breathed sighs of relief.

"Hey, Trix, none of that," Brian said gently as tears slid down her cheeks. "Everything's all right."

"I know," Trixie said. "It's just that I was so worried, and now I'm so happy. If anything ever happened to Reddy, Bobby would. . . ."

"And so would several other Beldens—me included," Brian told her. "Now, wipe away those tears, and we'll let Dr. Samet set Reddy's leg."

Brian assisted the doctor as he wrapped and set the broken leg. Soon they were finished, and Reddy was resting quietly.

"I have a dog bed in the back room, where he can sleep tonight," Dr. Samet said. "Brian, help me carry him. Come along," he added to Trixie and Miss Darcy. "I have some other little visitors I'd like you to meet."

"Could I call home first?" Trixie asked. "I'm sure they're all worried to death."

"Of course you can," Dr. Samet answered. "The phone's in my office."

Trixie dialed the number. The phone was picked up by her mother before it had finished ringing once.

Mrs. Belden breathed a sigh of relief as Trixie finished giving the doctor's report. "We haven't been able to get Bobby to calm down since Honey and Mart brought him home," she said. "I'll put him on, and you can tell him that Reddy will be okay."

Trixie reassured the still-sobbing Bobby, and then promised him that they would come to visit Reddy in the "hopsital" tomorrow. He had finally stopped crying by the time Trixie hung up.

Trixie made her way to the back room, where she found Brian, Dr. Samet, and Miss Darcy holding soft little kittens.

"Oh, they're adorable!" Trixie exclaimed as Dr. Samet handed her one of the black, fuzzy little balls.

"Don Morrison found this litter in the basement of his hardware store," Dr. Samet explained.

"The mother must have climbed in through one of the cellar windows. Then she either abandoned the kittens or went in search of food and couldn't get back in. Don looked for her for a while, and even left one of the windows open for a few days, but she never returned. They were too young to survive on their own, so he brought them here, and I've been playing nursemaid ever since. They're old enough to be on their own now, and I'm looking for good homes for them. Do you know of anyone who would like a kitten?" Dr. Samet asked.

"Brian, do you think—" Trixie began.

Brian looked doubtful. "I know exactly what you're thinking, Trixie, and I think you'd better clear it with Moms first. Also, we should wait until Reddy is settled at home again, or I'm afraid he'll think his spot as Number One Family Pet has been usurped."

"I suppose you're right," Trixie sighed. "This little guy is *so* cute, though. His nose is so tiny and pink; it looks like an eraser!"

"So it does," Miss Darcy laughed. "Actually, Dr. Samet, I was thinking about getting a pet. I was considering a watchdog, because I live alone, but a watch *kitten* would be cozier."

"You'd never have to worry about mice," Dr. Samet said, "but that's about as ferocious as any of these little rascals will ever get. Which one would you like?"

"I'd like the one I'm holding," Eileen Darcy answered, burying her face in the kitten's soft fur. Then she smiled at Dr. Samet. "And I think I'll name him after his 'nanny' and call him Sam."

"Sam it is, then, Miss . . . ?" The doctor ended on a questioning note.

"My goodness!" Trixie exclaimed. "We never even introduced you!"

"There were more important things to worry about when we first arrived, Trixie," Miss Darcy said kindly. Then she turned to the doctor and introduced herself.

"So you're the new drama teacher. I've heard about you," Dr. Samet said. "My niece, Jane Morgan, stops by every day and helps me feed the strays I pick up, and she was telling me about the production you're putting on."

"Jane Morgan is your niece?" Trixie exclaimed.

"Why, yes," Dr. Samet chuckled. "Is that so strange, Trixie, or aren't veterinarians supposed to have relatives? I'm not related to horses, you know," he teased. "My younger sister, Mary, is Jane's mother."

"I'm sorry, Dr. Samet," Trixie stammered. "I just never knew—"

"You'll have to excuse Trixie, Dr. Samet," Brian interrupted. "If *she* hasn't heard about something, then it must be something surprising or totally unimportant or mysterious." He nudged Trixie teasingly.

"Ah, yes, Trixie. I've heard that you seem to have a nose for mystery," the doctor said, not without admiration.

"Stronger than the best bloodhound you've ever seen," Brian chuckled.

"It's reassuring to know that Sleepyside has its own resident sleuth," Dr. Samet said.

Trixie blushed as she handed the little kitten back to Dr. Samet.

"Would you like to take your kitten with you now, Miss Darcy?" Dr. Samet tactfully turned the attention away from Trixie, sensing that she was embarrassed.

"I'd rather pick him up tomorrow," Eileen Darcy answered, "if that would be all right with you, Doctor. Then I could check up on how Reddy is doing, too."

"No problem. Just stop by anytime tomorrow afternoon."

Trixie and Brian tiptoed into the next room to check on Reddy and found him sleeping peacefully. Then Dr. Samet walked the trio to the door. They all thanked him repeatedly for his help as they bid the doctor good-night.

"He's a great guy—and a great veterinarian," Brian said as they headed toward the car.

"He certainly is," Miss Darcy agreed, taking the car keys that Brian handed her. "Thank you so much for driving, Brian." She smiled at him gratefully. "I'm quite recovered now, I think."

The trio climbed into the car. "I can't tell you how bad I feel about Reddy," Eileen Darcy said, starting the engine. "I'd like to apologize to your parents and to your little brother. I hope he isn't still so awfully upset. I'm sure the whole incident has given him quite a fright."

"I talked to him on the phone," Trixie said, "and he calmed down after hearing that Reddy was going to be all right."

They drove the rest of the way to Crabapple Farm in silence. Miss Darcy drove slowly, overly attentive to her driving.

Trixie, in the backseat again, was dying to

ask about the young teacher's father and the kidnapping, now that her mind was more at ease about Reddy. But she restrained herself, not wanting to upset Miss Darcy any more that evening.

When they finally reached Crabapple Farm, Mr. and Mrs. Belden, Mart, Honey, and Bobby were all anxiously waiting for them.

Brian introduced Miss Darcy, who immediately began apologizing for the accident. She insisted upon paying all the veterinarian bills.

"You're a bad lady!" Bobby cried, glaring at Eileen Darcy.

"Bobby!" Peter Belden said sharply. "We talked about this earlier, remember? It was an *accident*." He continued more gently. "You know that you should have gone to bed when you were told to, and you should not have taken Reddy out the way you did. I think you've learned your lesson tonight—the hard way. Now, young man, you owe Miss Darcy an apology."

Bobby's lower lip trembled as Miss Darcy stooped down to meet him at eye level. "Bobby," she explained slowly, "it *was* an accident, and I'm sorry—very, very sorry. But sometimes

59

things happen that we can't possibly know will happen. Dr. Samet says that Reddy will be all right and that he can come home in a couple of days. I hope we can still be friends," she said, extending her right hand.

Bobby stared at her for several moments and then finally nodded and shook her hand. "I'm sorry, too," he said in a small voice.

"Thank you, Bobby," Eileen Darcy said sincerely.

"Trixie, will you please take Bobby up to bed now?" Helen Belden asked.

"I should be going," Miss Darcy said. "I'll take Honey home and spend the night there."

"Miss Trask is waiting for us," Honey said. "I called her and told her what happened."

The Beldens bid Honey and Miss Darcy good-night and watched as they drove away.

"Whew! This certainly has been an eventful evening," Mart said, sighing.

"Yes, and it's time for *everyone* to get to bed," Mr. Belden added.

Upstairs, Trixie tucked Bobby into bed, assuring him that Reddy was sound asleep and that his leg wasn't "hurting awfully." She was exhausted, but she sat with him until he went to sleep, which didn't take the overtired little boy very long. *Poor kid*, Trixie thought, kissing his cheek. *This must have been one of the roughest nights of his life. Maybe of mine, too*. She sighed and headed for her own room.

Tired as she was, she couldn't help going over the evening's events while she was undressing. She frowned, wondering why Miss Darcy had decided to drive all the way out there on such a snowy night, especially when she had already told Miss Trask she wasn't coming. *And that letter*, Trixie thought. *Who gets mail that late in the evening?*

Then she sighed wearily and climbed into bed. *Stop asking yourself all those questions*, Trixie reprimanded herself, *or you'll never get to sleep. And maybe you're just being nosy*, she thought, cringing at the memory of Jane Morgan's words. *But still. . . .*

First Rehearsal • 4

ALL THE BELDENS had a difficult time believing that morning had come so soon when their alarms sounded at 7:00 A.M.—all, that is, except Bobby. Mr. Belden, who woke up early to start the morning coffee, found Bobby in the kitchen packing Reddy's toys and dog food in a small suitcase.

"What *are* you doing?" Peter Belden asked sleepily.

"I'm getting ready to visit Reddy in the hopsital. He needs his food and his ball and his. . . ."

"Hold on there, young man!" Mr. Belden

laughed. "Reddy's in the hospital to rest, and Dr. Samet has food there for him. Besides, you have to go to school first. Then your mother will take you to visit Reddy."

"But, Daddy. . . ."

"No buts, ands, or anything. Now go get ready for school," Mr. Belden said, smiling at his youngest son.

"Aw, shucks," Bobby mumbled to himself and slowly started up the stairs. "What if Reddy forgets all about me?" he called over his shoulder.

"Who could forget you, half-pint?" Mart called down the stairs. "Especially when you're making such a racket so early in the morning!"

Soon all the Beldens were up and seated at the breakfast table. "I'm going to call Dr. Samet before we leave for school, to check on Reddy," Trixie said.

"Can I talk to Reddy," Bobby asked, "so I can tell him I'm coming to visit?"

"I don't think Reddy will be able to come to the phone," Trixie chuckled, "but I'll ask Dr. Samet to tell him."

"You'd better hurry up. You're running behind this morning, and the bus will be here soon," Mrs. Belden told her three eldest children. "In fact, *soon* is the wrong word—*now* is more appropriate," she said, glancing out the window.

Trixie, Brian, and Mart raced for their hats, coats, and gloves.

"All these arctic accoutrements are so burdensome," Mart complained, pulling on his boots.

"Phone the vet from school, if you want to," Mrs. Belden called after the trio as they raced to meet their bus. "And have a nice day!"

Trixie collapsed on the seat across from Honey and Di, who both immediately asked about Reddy.

"I told Di the whole story, of course," Honey said.

"I didn't have time to call Dr. Samet this morning, but I'll call him from school." Trixie sat up straight suddenly. "Honey, I thought you and Jim would be riding to school with Miss Darcy. Didn't she stay over last night?"

"She got up very early this morning and drove back into town," Honey answered. "Maybe she had to get some things ready for our first rehearsal."

"Don't remind me," Di groaned. "After I talked to you last night, Trixie, all I did was practice, practice, practice! I think I'm going to be saying 'O Romeo, Romeo! wherefore art thou Romeo?' in my sleep!"

"I'm excited about the costumes," Honey said. "I wonder if we'll be renting some or making all of them."

"You know," Trixie admitted, "I'm a stagehand, but I'm afraid I don't even know what a stagehand *does*!"

Mart groaned from the seat behind her, then snorted rudely. Turning to Brian and Jim, he spouted pompously, "I ask you, members of the jury, is this not a misrepresentation on the part of Beatrix Belden—to feign knowledge of a special skill of which she is totally ignorant? It's villainous! This young woman is completely incorrigible!"

"Fortunately for you, Mart Belden, I have better things to do than to eavesdrop on other people's conversations. Obviously, you do not," Trixie retorted smartly as the bus pulled up in front of Sleepyside Junior-Senior High. She gathered up her books and stalked off the bus, followed by Honey and Di.

"You can't win 'em all." Mart shrugged and filed out behind them.

In between two of her morning classes, Trixie called Dr. Samet's office and learned that Reddy was doing fine.

Drama class was held just before lunch hour. The group of anxious freshmen gathered in the school auditorium for their first rehearsal. Eileen Darcy arrived looking tense and tired, but she smiled as she faced the class from the stage.

"We are very fortunate," Miss Darcy announced, "in that we will not have to make or rent most of the costumes for this production. A friend of mine," she went on to explain, "is the proprietor of a costume company in London, and she is planning a show in New York City.

"She has offered to send some of her Shakespearean costumes ahead for us to use, free of charge—which will certainly help our meager costume budget," Miss Darcy added.

"Now, to begin, putting on a play is a serious business. Anyone who thinks this will simply be a time to chat with his friends or to lounge about can do us all a favor and leave right now.

A play is certainly a great deal of fun, but it is also a good bit of work," she finished.

The entire class sat quietly and listened attentively. "Good," Miss Darcy said. "Now that that obligatory speech is over, we can *really* begin." She smiled, and the class smiled and relaxed, too.

"First, I'll be dividing you all into groups. The senior aides will assign the stagehands to different crews. We will need one crew for scenery and another for props. The costume crew will be divided into wardrobe and makeup crews. The lighting crew will be under the supervision of senior aide Jenny Ratner.

"I have asked the art club to help design posters and programs and to help paint scenery. But before we get to work on those things, I want you all to understand some basic stage geography. I am passing out a mimeographed diagram of the stage area, and I want you all to memorize it. You must be as familiar with the layout of the stage as you are with that of your own house. We can't have people running into each other or not knowing where a prop has to be at a certain time."

They all listened carefully while Miss Darcy

67

explained that downstage is closest to the audience and upstage is farthest away. *Stage right*
means to your right as you stand on the stage
facing the audience, she told them, and the
wings are the areas on either side of the stage,
most of the time hidden by parts of the scenery.

"When you 'wait in the wings,' " Miss Darcy
explained, "you're waiting in one or the other
of those areas, either as an actor or actress
ready to enter, or as a stagehand with a prop or
a change of costume."

The divided grid of the stage, as shown on the
diagram, looked very confusing to most of the
students until the drama teacher explained that
U.R. entrance meant that the actor or actress
came onto the stage from the upstage-right entrance. The stage was divided into quadrants
marked *up right* and *down right*, and *up center*
and *down center*, and *up left* and *down left*.

Di leaned over and whispered to Honey.
"This all seems so confusing. Not only do I have
to memorize all those lines, but now I've got to
remember where I'm supposed to say them
from!"

"Do you have a question, Miss Lynch?"
Eileen Darcy snapped. "If you do, I wish you'd

direct it to me. An actress *must* know all these things."

Di blushed a bright red and apologized. Jane Morgan giggled from a seat somewhere behind Di. Trixie, sitting next to Honey on the other side, turned and glared at Jane.

I'd better keep an eye on her, Trixie thought as she and Honey exchanged knowing looks.

Miss Darcy's mood changed suddenly. She rubbed her forehead nervously. "I—I'm sorry," she began. "I'm a little on edge today. I know this must all look very confusing to you, but it will become much clearer once we start the rehearsals.

"All right," she said briskly. "Costume crew over there." She motioned to her left. "Stagehands next to them, and lighting crew over there." Students quickly gathered in their assigned places. "All actors and actresses remain—" Miss Darcy broke off suddenly, then finished her sentence absentmindedly, "—seated." She paused. "Excuse me, class, I'll be right back." She walked quickly to the back of the auditorium, where Peter Ashbury, her fiancé, was standing.

Trixie poked Honey in the ribs. "There's

69

'dreamboat,' " she whispered. "I wonder what he's doing here during school hours."

"Maybe he came to take Miss Darcy to lunch," Honey suggested.

"She certainly seems nervous this morning," Trixie mused, "but it's perfectly understandable. She must be terribly worried about her father." Honey giggled. "What's so funny about that?" Trixie asked.

"That's not funny," Honey answered. "It was your 'perfectly understandable' that made me laugh. Everything has to be at least 'understandable' with you, if not *'perfectly* understandable.' "

Trixie giggled, too. "I guess you're right, Honey. But you know that detectives have to think like that all the time, not just when they're working on a case!"

Suddenly Jane Morgan interrupted the whispered conversation.

"I heard Miss Darcy spent last night at your house, Honey," Jane said, a stiff smile fixed on her face. "You're getting pretty chummy with a teacher, inviting her over for a slumber party." She sniffed.

"Miss Darcy came to visit Miss Trask, not Honey," Trixie answered sharply.

70

"Oh, yes, her *governess*. Well, not everyone has a governess that happens to be friends with one of the teachers," Jane observed, with a snide smile.

"It just so happens that—" Trixie began.

"I know the whole story, Trixie Belden," Jane interjected, all pretense of a smile gone. "You know, you and your gang aren't the only ones who are privileged with certain information."

Honey spoke before Trixie could respond again. "That's true, Jane," she answered sweetly and then quickly turned away from the girl.

"She's just jealous," Honey said under her breath to Trixie. "Don't let it get you so upset. I *do* wonder how she knew about last night, though."

Trixie's face was red with anger. "I forgot to tell you," she said. "Jane is Dr. Samet's niece. She helps him with the animals. She probably went to help him before school this morning, and he must have told her what happened last night. She makes me so mad!"

"I know," Honey said, "but you've got to try to ignore her."

The class was beginning to get restless as Miss Darcy returned from talking with her fiancé.

Trixie turned and saw him waiting at the back of the auditorium.

"We only have a couple of minutes left before the bell," Miss Darcy said loudly. "I want you all to come back here right after lunch, and we'll discuss your assignments for tomorrow." Then Miss Darcy dismissed the class.

As students filed out of the auditorium, Honey, Trixie, and Di passed very near Peter Ashbury. They'd gone only a short distance down the hallway when Honey suddenly stopped.

"What's wrong, Honey?" Trixie asked.

"I think I've seen that man somewhere before," she mused aloud.

"Of course you have, Honey," Trixie said, puzzled. "You've seen him pick Miss Darcy up after school lots of times!"

"I know, but I've seen him somewhere else, too. I just realized it, but I can't remember where."

"*Now* who needs to have everything 'perfectly understandable'?" Trixie laughed.

"I know," Honey said. "I'm getting as bad as you. It's probably nothing, but I *know* I've seen him before—somewhere. . . ."

The Costumes From England · 5

THE FIRST FEW DAYS of rehearsal went smoothly. "Work downstage," "Stay to the center line," and "Exit stage left" now made some sense to the cast and crew, who eagerly worked together under Eileen Darcy's direction.

Trixie, up to her elbows in paint, was carefully filling in a backdrop for one of the scenes. "I never imagined there was so much work to do!" she exclaimed to Jim Frayne, who was working beside her. He had volunteered as one of the senior aides to help with scenery and posters.

"This is just the beginning, Trixie," Jim told

73

her. "Wait until you have to have all the props ready and the scenes set up on time. But you'll have a shift chart for that," he added.

"A shift chart?"

"Sure," Jim answered. "Stagehands work in pairs, because things have to be set up and taken down quickly between scenes. You and your partner will be assigned things to do in a certain order. Let's say that one scene calls for a chair and the next one doesn't. Your shift chart will say 'set chair' for that first scene and 'strike chair' for the next scene."

"Oh," Trixie said. "I should have guessed what it meant. You know, Jim," she continued more cheerfully, "this is really a lot of fun. Everyone is working together, helping each other. I like it."

"Maybe you'll change your career plans," Jim teased, "and take up set designing."

"Never!" Trixie laughed. "I don't like it *that* much."

They finished the backdrop and quickly cleaned up. On the way back to the auditorium, they stopped in the wardrobe room to see how Honey was doing. As they approached, they could hear Jane Morgan's voice.

"Honey Wheeler, you took this in *too* much. Now look at how it fits her!" Jane was pointing to a costume worn by one of the girls in the cast.

"Why, Jane," Trixie said innocently as she entered the room, "I didn't know *you* were in charge of the costume crew."

"I'm not," Jane snapped back, "but someone has to keep an eye on all these people who don't know what they're doing. We have to make *some* of the costumes, you know. It seems only *Juliet* gets the special ones from England."

Trixie held her temper with difficulty. She turned to Honey. "It's almost time for lunch, Honey. Why don't you come out in front with us and watch the end of the rehearsal?"

Honey nodded, picked up her sewing equipment, and walked out with them.

"Whew! I wouldn't want to get on her bad side," Jim whistled when they were out of earshot. "What did you do to her, Honey, stick her with a needle?"

"She should have!" Trixie exclaimed. She explained to Jim that Jane was jealous of Di for getting the part of Juliet and that she seemed to be taking it out on everyone else.

"But honestly, Honey, I don't know how you can tolerate her!" Trixie said, exasperated. " 'Too long, too short, too tight. . . .' She's just doing that to aggravate you."

"I know," Honey responded, "but jealousy can sometimes make people do strange things. I don't think Jane really means to be that way."

"Of course she does!" Trixie retorted. "Honey, you're just too nice sometimes. You're always trying to see the good side of people, and usually they end up taking advantage of you."

Trixie became silent as they entered the auditorium and slipped into front row seats. The cast was working on Act II, Scene II, in which Juliet speaks to Romeo from her balcony window.

Miss Darcy still seemed very much on edge, and according to Miss Trask, who spoke to the drama teacher daily, there was still no word about her father. Peter Ashbury came to rehearsals every day and sat quietly in the back of the auditorium until lunch break.

Trixie watched her pretty friend rehearse the part of Juliet.

" 'Good-night, good-night! parting is such sweet sorrow. . . .' " Di faltered and stopped.

She blushed a deep red, then stammered through the line again, repeating "sweet sorrow" several times.

"Well, Diana?" Miss Darcy demanded impatiently, her voice sharp.

Poor Di, Trixie groaned inwardly.

Suddenly a voice was heard from the wings. " 'That I shall say good-night till it be morrow.' "

"That's Jane Morgan!" Trixie hissed to Honey and Jim.

"Thank you, Jane," Miss Darcy was saying. "*Try* to remember your lines, Diana! That's the second time today that Jane has had to help you. There won't be any prompting on the night of the performance," she admonished curtly.

Eileen Darcy was interrupted just then by a student bearing a message from the principal's office. After reading it, her mood suddenly changed.

"The costumes from England have arrived." Miss Darcy's face was flushed, and she seemed very excited. "If everyone is willing to forego a few minutes of their lunch break, I'll bring them in and we'll take a look at them."

All the students agreed. Miss Darcy asked for several volunteers to help carry the boxes. Jim and Trixie quickly offered, and they headed toward the office with Miss Darcy. On their way out, Peter Ashbury rose and offered to help, too.

There were three large, flat boxes. Jim carried one, Ashbury another, and Trixie and Eileen Darcy carried the third. They took them back to the auditorium and set them on the stage.

Trixie immediately began opening one of the boxes. "What do you think you're doing?" Peter Ashbury demanded. "I think you should wait until you're asked to do something. Perhaps Miss Darcy would like to open them. They are her responsibility, after all."

"I—I was only trying to help," Trixie stammered, blushing furiously.

"Mr. Ashbury is right, Trixie," Miss Darcy said smoothly. "I would like to open them myself, since they are on loan to us."

She quickly began opening the boxes as the students looked on. The first costume she removed was a beautiful cape.

"This is to be worn by Romeo in the first act," she explained. She then proceeded to remove the rest of the costumes, until finally she brought out a long, exquisite velvet gown with intricate lace and jewel designs.

"This is lovely!" she exclaimed, holding up the gown.

Suddenly a flashbulb went off. Eileen Darcy looked up in surprise.

"Didn't mean to startle you, Miss Darcy," said the smiling young man with the camera. "I just wanted to get some shots for the paper, and I think candid ones are often the best." It was Bill Morgan, Jane's older brother, who was a photographer for the school newspaper. "I plan to do a whole article about the play," he explained glibly.

"That's fine," Eileen Darcy said. "You just startled me, that's all." Then she glanced down at her wristwatch. "I've detained you long enough, class. You'd better get to lunch. Mr. Ashbury and I will carry the costumes to my office. And, Trixie, after lunch, will you please stop in and see me for a few minutes?"

Trixie nodded, then gathered her things and walked to the cafeteria with Di, Jim, and Honey.

"It looks like we've all gotten in some hot water today," Trixie sighed. "Jane yelled at Honey, Di forgot a line, Mr. Ashbury snapped at me, and now Miss Darcy wants to see me. I wonder what else I did! Is there a full moon or something?''

"Maybe it's hunting season for Bob-Whites," Honey giggled.

Trixie laughed, too, and then became serious again. "Did you notice how nervous Miss Darcy was while she was opening the costumes?"

"She's been nervous all week," Jim said, "and that really doesn't need any explanation, Trixie. She's undoubtedly worried about her father, and maybe she's still shaken by the accident with Reddy."

Throughout the walk to the cafeteria, Di had been unusually quiet. "Is something wrong, Di?" Honey finally asked.

"No . . . well, yes," Di began, tears filling her violet-colored eyes. She hesitated for a moment, then blurted out, "I don't think I can play Juliet! All the lines I knew yesterday, I've forgotten today, and the ones I'll have to learn for tomorrow, I'll probably forget by the next day! Jane knows all of them. Maybe *she* should play the part."

"Don't be ridic, Di!" Trixie exclaimed angrily. "Sure she knows the play—she's probably got a script in her hand, waiting for you to forget a line. And *she's* not out there saying them in front of all those people!"

"Trixie's right," Honey added firmly. "Tomorrow's Friday—we'll help you practice all weekend. You're going to do just fine."

"I agree with both of them," Jim said, handing Di a handkerchief. "Now, dry those eyes, and let's eat, or you'll be too weak from hunger to go back to rehearsal."

Brian and Mart were already seated at a table and were half-finished with their sandwiches by the time Honey, Di, Trixie, and Jim joined them.

"What detained thee, thespian friends and sibling?" Mart asked blithely.

"The costumes from England arrived," Honey answered, "and we all stayed to see them. There are some beautiful gowns that Di will get to wear."

"They are lovely, aren't they?" Di said, brightening a little.

It was Trixie's turn to be quiet. She silently munched her sandwich as her friends chattered on about the play and costumes.

"Uh-oh," Mart said. "I get the feeling that

this is the lull before the storm. What's brewing in that cranial cauldron, Trix?"

"I'm just thinking instead of gabbing, for once," she answered flippantly, getting up and quickly gathering her books. "And I've got to run. Miss Darcy wants to see me before rehearsal." She left the lunchroom abruptly.

Mart whistled softly. "What's with Trixie? That's the quietest I've seen her since birth. She's not onto some mystery, is she?" he asked Honey.

"No," Honey laughed, "not that I know of, anyway."

"You'd be the first to hear if she was," Brian said, "so I guess we can all rest easy for a while."

Trixie knocked softly on Miss Darcy's office door, but there was no answer. *She must have gone out to eat*, Trixie thought. The door was slightly ajar, so she let herself in.

Trixie looked around the small office. Many interesting posters advertising London and Broadway plays hung on the walls. One, for a London production of *Romeo and Juliet*, depicted Juliet standing on a balcony wearing a dress very similar to the velvet gown sent from England. Trixie wondered if Miss Darcy's friend had designed that one, too.

She sat down to wait for the drama teacher. She picked up a catalog that she found on a small table next to the chair. *Honey and Di would love to see these costumes*, Trixie thought, flipping through the catalog, which was entitled *The Shakespearean Costume Guide.*

Suddenly the door flew open, and in walked Peter Ashbury. Trixie jumped at the sudden intrusion, nearly dropping the catalog she'd been looking at. A deep scowl creased Ashbury's forehead.

"Now what are you doing?" he growled. "Snooping around, I suppose." He snatched the catalog from her hands. "Someone should teach you some manners!"

Trixie, momentarily flustered, stumbled through an apology. "I— Miss Darcy wanted to see me. I was just waiting for her. The door was open."

"She'll be here in a minute," he said sullenly.

Trixie, completely puzzled by his outburst, was now suddenly angry. "I don't know why you're shouting at me," she said indignantly. "I

83

didn't do anything wrong."

Just then Eileen Darcy came into the room. "What's going on here?" she demanded. "I could hear you all the way down the hall."

Ashbury answered before Trixie could say a word. "I came in here and caught her," he said, pointing an accusing finger, "going through your things."

"Trixie!" Miss Darcy exclaimed.

"I was just looking through the costume catalog that was set out on your table," Trixie explained. Her anger was gone, but she was more puzzled than ever. "The door was open. You told me you wanted to see me, Miss Darcy. I was just waiting for you."

"That's true. I did ask you to stop in before rehearsal, didn't I?" Eileen Darcy ran her fingers through her hair distractedly. Then she said, "Oh! Yes. I spoke to Dr. Samet this morning. He assured me that Reddy would be fine and that he'll be able to go home tomorrow. It seems that when your mother and Bobby visited him yesterday, your mother paid the veterinarian's bill. I do want to reimburse her, so would you please give her this check?" she asked, handing Trixie an envelope. "And please tell your family, especially Bobby, how sorry I am."

"Of course," Trixie answered, accepting the envelope.

"I'll see you at rehearsal in a few minutes," Miss Darcy added. As Trixie left, she glanced back and saw the drama teacher give Peter Ashbury a cool look.

There's something very strange going on here, Trixie thought as she closed the office door behind her. She was about to start walking toward the auditorium, when she heard Peter Ashbury and Eileen Darcy's voices rise in angry tones.

I know I shouldn't eavesdrop, Trixie thought. Common sense told her to leave quietly, but her curiosity about what was going on was stronger, and she stayed.

"Where did you disappear to earlier?" she heard Miss Darcy ask. "I had to have some of the students help me carry the costumes back here, and then I spent the rest of the time looking for you. I thought we were supposed to have lunch together. And then, when I finally did find you, you were shouting at one of my students!"

"I had some errands to do."

"Errands? What kind of errands do you have at noon in a high school?"

"Listen, Eileen, if you don't want me around here, just say so. Work is slow now, and with your father missing, I thought you might appreciate having me around more often. I don't *have* to drive up from New York City every day, you know. And now that. . . ."

"Now that what?" Miss Darcy demanded quietly. To Trixie's ears, the drama teacher's tone sounded ominous.

"Now that—now that you think I'm interfering with your work, I won't bother coming!" he said with finality. Trixie heard footsteps approaching on the other side of the door, so she quickly tiptoed to the next classroom and slipped inside. She heard the office door open and then close with a resounding slam. She waited until she could no longer hear the heavy footsteps receding down the hall. Then she hurried to the auditorium for rehearsal.

The rest of the class was already there, waiting for Miss Darcy. Trixie scanned the group, looking for Honey; not seeing her, she hurried to the wardrobe room backstage.

"What's wrong?" Honey asked immediately,

seeing the look on Trixie's face.

"I'll tell you after school," Trixie whispered, catching Jane Morgan's hostile, inquisitive glance.

"I've got to get back to the auditorium. Miss Darcy will be here any minute," Trixie said. "I just wanted to see if you had a second to talk, but I guess not," Trixie added, rolling her eyes toward Jane.

"I understand," Honey said. "I've got some things to tell you, too!"

Trixie ran back to the auditorium, arriving just as Miss Darcy walked in. The drama teacher's eyes were red and puffy—she looked as if she had been crying.

"I'm sorry I'm late, class," she apologized. "We only have twenty-five minutes left in this period, but we'll start where we left off before lunch. Diana, will you please begin? All stage-hands, please assemble in the wings. Jeff Hoffer will show you how to work the equipment for the backdrops you've been painting."

After rehearsal, the rest of the afternoon seemed to drag on and on. Trixie couldn't concentrate on Napoleon during history class or on *The Grapes of Wrath*—although she enjoyed the book—during English. She was so preoccupied with the day's events that everything else seemed to pale next to them.

Finally, the dismissal bell for the last class rang, and Trixie hurried to meet Honey and the rest of the Bob-Whites in front of school to wait for the school bus.

"Honey," she asked anxiously, "why don't you come home with me tonight? I'm sure Moms will be glad to have you for dinner, and I've just *got* to talk to you—privately!"

"Buzz, buzz, buzz—the sound only an apiculturist loves," Mart laughed. "Now what are you two busy bees buzzing about?"

"Afraid you're missing out on something?" Trixie asked coyly.

"No," Mart began, "but you've been acting strangely all day, Trixie. I hope you're not into one of your maybe-this-or-maybe-that wild-goose chases."

"Not at all." Trixie laughed lightly and boarded the bus.

They all chattered happily on the way home, and as they neared Crabapple Farm, Honey said that she would go home first and ask Miss Trask if she could spend the night.

Mart, Brian, and Trixie were met at the door by Bobby. "Guess what, guess what?" the little boy demanded, jumping up and down excitedly. "Reddy's coming home tomorrow!"

"So I heard," Trixie said, giving Bobby a hug and a kiss.

"Oh, did you call Dr. Samet today?" her mother asked.

"No, but Miss Darcy did, and she told me," Trixie replied. Then she took out the envelope Miss Darcy had given her and handed it to her mother. "She also asked me to give you this check."

"I told her that wasn't necessary," Helen Belden said, opening the envelope. "Why, this isn't a check, Trixie. This is a receipt for a safe-deposit box—and some pictures of costumes!"

"It is?" Trixie asked, her eyes widening.

"She must have given you the wrong envelope. Will you return this to her tomorrow?" Mrs. Belden asked. She handed the envelope back to Trixie.

"Sure, Moms," Trixie answered, trying to contain her excitement. "Oh, Moms, can Honey have dinner with us and then spend the night?"

"Honey is welcome for dinner any night, but

you know how I feel about friends sleeping over during the school week," her mother answered.

"I know, Moms. But just this once, please?" Trixie pleaded. "We have something important to discuss."

"One of these days, you're going to use up your quota of 'just this onces,' " Mrs. Belden laughed, "but I suppose it's all right—'just this once.' "

"Thanks, Moms! You're super! And I promise we won't stay up late."

"What's so important that it has to be discussed tonight?" Mrs. Belden asked.

"You know better than to ask Trixie to divulge her *important* business, Moms," Brian laughed.

But Trixie didn't hear them—she was already on her way upstairs, the envelope clutched tightly in her hand.

Strange Happenings • 6

HONEY CALLED to say that Miss Trask had given her permission to spend the night, on the condition that she finish her homework first.

"Well, hurry up and finish," Trixie said urgently, "and then come right over. I'll finish my drudgery, too, and then it'll all be out of the way." She said good-bye and hung up the phone.

Less than an hour later, Honey arrived with her overnight case. Trixie was upstairs, finishing the last of her algebra problems, when she heard Bobby's enthusiastic welcome.

Trixie slammed her book shut, raced down the stairs, and began to literally drag Honey toward the stairway.

"Sorry, everyone," Trixie called over her shoulder. "You can talk to her at dinner!"

"What *is* going on?" Trixie heard her mother ask Mart, who was in the process of raiding the cookie jar.

"It's either one of Trixie's clever ways of getting out of work—in this case, setting the table —or there's been some *terrible* catastrophe. For as long as I live, Moms, I'll never understand teen-age girls or aspiring detectives, especially if you combine the two. Then you've got a really volatile mixture!"

"On that point, I agree with you, Mart," Mrs. Belden said, laughing. "And I'm glad you brought up the matter of setting the table, because that's exactly what needs to be done, as soon as you're done with the cookies."

"Me and my big mouth," Mart groaned.

Upstairs, Honey and Trixie sat side by side on Trixie's bed.

"Finally!" Trixie exclaimed. "I've been on the verge of bursting all day long, waiting to talk to you."

"Me, too," Honey said. "Do you want to go first, or should I?"

"You first," Trixie said anxiously.

"Okay," Honey began. "After you left the lunchroom, I took a couple of minutes to go to the library to get some of those new history pamphlets. And. . . ."

"Honey!" Trixie cried with exasperation. "Tell the story!"

Honey giggled. "Sometimes I do get side-tracked. After I got the pamphlets, I was walking back to my locker, and I saw Mr. Ashbury talking with Bill and Jane Morgan in front of the newspaper office. I thought it seemed a little bit funny that he would be talking to them, and I was still bothered about where I had seen Mr. Ashbury before, so I turned down the side corridor and listened."

"Honey!" Trixie exclaimed, pretending to be shocked. "I'm surprised at you! *I'm* usually the one who does that sort of thing and gets scolded by *you*."

"I know," Honey laughed. "It must be getting into my blood! Anyway," she continued, "they were talking about the photographs that Bill took of the costumes today. Mr. Ashbury asked Bill for copies of the pictures, and then he gave him his address. I didn't hear all of it—just New York City—and then I suddenly remembered where I had seen Peter Ashbury before!"

Trixie was leaning forward, listening eagerly to every word and trying to piece this new information into the patchwork of things she had so far.

"Mother was helping with a Halloween benefit dinner last October for some club in New York," Honey continued, "and I went into the city with her one day. One of the stops we made was at a costume company, and I'm almost certain that Peter Ashbury was the man who helped her. We were there for quite a while, and I remember looking at a lot of the costumes. I asked Miss Trask about it, but she said she didn't know what kind of work Mr. Ashbury did. And Mother and Daddy left for Miami last night and won't be back until next week, so I can't ask Mother if she remembers him.

"After Bill and Jane and Mr. Ashbury finished talking," Honey continued, "I waited a few minutes and then headed back to the auditorium for rehearsal. I saw Jane and Bill in the hallway, but Mr. Ashbury wasn't with them."

"Unfortunately, *I* know where he was," Trixie interrupted. "But I'll tell you that later. Then what happened?"

"I walked behind Bill and Jane for a few minutes. They didn't see me at first. Bill said that he was going to do a whole article on the play, with pictures of Di and the rest of the cast in Shakespearean costume. Jane said that he'd better wait to take the pictures, because Di wasn't going to be playing Juliet!

"Unfortunately, Jane turned her head just then and saw that I was following them, so she stopped talking. She whispered something to Bill and then, very nicely, offered to walk to the auditorium with me. I didn't let on that I had heard her, but I was seething!"

"Whew!" Trixie exclaimed. "This gets stranger and stranger!" Then she related the whole story of what had happened in the drama office, including the argument she had overheard between Miss Darcy and Peter Ashbury.

"And now this!" With a flourish, Trixie produced the envelope containing the pictures and safe-deposit box receipt.

Honey looked at them quizzically. "What do these have to do with the rest of it?" she asked.

"I must admit I don't know yet," Trixie answered slowly. She explained to Honey about Miss Darcy giving her the wrong envelope.

"Something very strange is going on here," Trixie sighed. "Remember how upset Mr. Ashbury got when I started opening the costume boxes at rehearsal? Maybe—if he *is* in the business—he wants to steal them. Maybe they're very valuable costumes, and that's why Miss Darcy is going to keep them in a safe-deposit box!"

"Trixie," Honey laughed, "safe-deposit boxes are too small for costumes. They're for things like jewelry and valuable papers, not clothes!"

"Oh," Trixie said. "But what about fur coats? They're valuable. Where do people keep them in summer?"

"Certainly not in safe-deposit boxes!" Honey said. "In the summer, my mother has hers stored in a furrier's vault."

"Well, scratch that explanation," Trixie sighed. "Jane Morgan worries me, too. I wonder if we should tell Di about this. That's the second time Jane's said something threatening about Di playing Juliet. Maybe Jane plans to kidnap Di on the night of the performance!"

Trixie said, her eyes widening.

"Oh, Trixie, Jane wouldn't go that far!" Honey rolled her eyes.

"I don't know about that," Trixie began, but she was interrupted by Mrs. Belden's call for dinner.

"Uh-oh," Trixie groaned. "I'll probably get a talking-to about chores, plus some ribbing from Mart, who probably ended up setting the table for me."

Just as Trixie had predicted, Mart gave her a hard time once they were all seated at the dining room table.

"Did you solve all the world's problems while I did your work, Trixie?" Mart asked.

"Almost," Trixie answered. "We've got just one problem left: what to do about older brothers."

"Now, now," Peter Belden interjected. "Let's try to have a peaceful dinner—and, I hope, a calmer evening than the last one Honey spent with us."

"That reminds me, Peter," Helen Belden said. "Reddy can come home tomorrow. I thought Brian could drive everyone to school, and then they can pick Reddy up on their way home. I've got a lot of work to do tomorrow, and I won't have time to drive into town."

"That's fine with me," Brian said. "I know someone here who will sure be glad to welcome Reddy home," he added, ruffling Bobby's hair.

"I've got everything all set," Bobby said. "I'm going to sign Reddy's cast."

"You're going to do *what*?" Mr. Belden asked.

"When Jimmy Baker broked his arm," Bobby explained patiently, "everyone in my class got to sign his cast. I remember how to do it, so I'm going to sign Reddy's."

"Well, we'll see," Mr. Belden said, chuckling. "You know, Bobby, you're going to have to let Reddy rest a lot."

"I know. I checked out some libarry books this week, so I can read him lots and lots of stories. Trixie can help me with the words. Right, Trixie?"

"Sure, half-pint," Trixie answered, smiling down at her little brother. "Let's start with how to pronounce 'library.' "

They were just finishing dessert when the telephone rang. "I'll get it," Trixie said, jumping up.

"It never fails," Mart groaned. "Right on cue—just when it's time to do dishes!"

"I'll help tonight," Honey said. "Thank you very much for the delicious dinner, Mr. and Mrs. Belden."

Trixie was gone only a few minutes before coming back to the table.

"Shortest conversation you've ever had, Trix. What was it, a wrong number?" Mart teased.

"Nope," Trixie answered. "Wrong envelope. It was Miss Darcy. She was so embarrassed about giving me the wrong envelope. I told her I would return it tomorrow morning and pick up the right one. That was all." Trixie shrugged, but she gave Honey a knowing look.

Mr. and Mrs. Belden went into the living room to read the evening paper. Honey, Trixie, Brian, and Mart cleared the table and started the dishes.

Bobby wanted to "help," but Mart quickly diverted him by suggesting that he make a welcome-home sign for Reddy. Soon Bobby was stationed at the dining room table, eagerly at work with paper and crayons.

"Okay, Trixie, what's going on?" Mart and Brian demanded in unison.

"Whatever could you mean, dear brothers?" Trixie asked innocently, suddenly very interested in an imaginary spot on a plate she was drying.

"Neither of us is deaf, dumb, or blind," Brian said, "and we know how you work."

"Unfortunately," Mart added.

"So what's up?" Brian pursued. "I suppose you found Eileen Darcy's father bound and gagged in some hotel room in White Plains, or something equally incredible."

"No, but I wish I had," Trixie answered, with a rueful smile. "Well, Honey, what do you think—shall we tell them?"

"There's really not that much to tell," Honey said. "At least, nothing that makes any sense. It's such a hodgepodge right now."

"That's not hard to believe," Brian said. "I just don't want you two getting yourselves into some kind of trouble and then not being able to get out of it—especially when you leave us in the dark."

"So you'd better start, Trixie, or we'll have to use some drastic methods, like dragging you outside and throwing you in a snowbank," Mart threatened.

100

Trixie gave up and told the whole story, both Honey's experiences and her own, ending with the mix-up of the envelopes.

When she had finished, Mart said, "And?"

"And nothing. That's it," Trixie answered.

Mart hooted. "This is the best one so far, Trixie! Some schoolgirl shamus you are! You should stick to your schoolwork and chores. If you did those the way you're supposed to, you wouldn't have time for all this craziness!"

"Mart, you have no imagination!" Trixie exclaimed, exasperated.

"Thank goodness!" Mart laughed. "One imagination is enough for this family. Look, Trixie," he added more seriously, "all you've got is one very upset drama teacher whose father has been kidnapped—in England, remember. Then you've got one overprotective boyfriend who likes to come to rehearsals and is interested in some pictures of costumes. No harm in that. Then you're left with one jealous classmate who has harassed people, so far, but really hasn't *done* anything. Now, if you can legitimately put that together into some kind of mystery, I'll eat a whale."

"That's no dare, Mart Belden. You'd eat

anything." Trixie laughed, but she had a determined look on her face.

Brian had been quiet throughout the telling of the story, but now he gave his opinion. "I don't know, Mart, the whole thing sounds a little fishy to me, too—no reference to your dinner plans intended."

Mart retorted, "A whale isn't a fish, it's a—"

"I know, I know," Brian laughed. "But fishy or not, I'd like to take a look at that safe-deposit receipt and those pictures, Trixie."

"Oh, no!" Mart groaned. "I can't believe you're falling for any of this, Brian. And I used to think you were so level-headed."

For all of Mart's pooh-poohing, he accompanied the others up to Trixie's room to look at the contents of the envelope.

"Hmmm," Brian mused, looking at the pictures. "I thought you said these were photographs, Trixie. They're not. These are pictures from a book. Look—there's printing on the back of them."

"Or from a catalog!" Trixie exclaimed. "Let me see those again." Brian handed her the pictures. "There are six of them. Honey, do you know how many costumes were delivered?"

"Six, I think. Let me see, there was the velvet gown, the cape, and another costume for Romeo, and three more dresses. Yes, six in all."

"Now, look at these pictures again, Honey," Trixie directed. "Are these the same six costumes? I wish I had paid more attention to them! All I remember is the velvet gown, and here's the picture of that."

"I think they're the same," Honey said, "but I'm not positive."

"You know, Trixie, even if these are the same costumes," Mart said, "it could be that Miss Darcy's friend sent the pictures earlier, just to show her what the costumes looked like."

"That's true," Brian put in, "and she may have a safe-deposit box for any number of reasons—her passport and birth certificate, just to name two. Lots of people have one for documents.

"What we're trying to say, Trixie, is that your 'mystery' can be easily explained. Your worst problem, if you insist upon having one, is Jane Morgan, and she's easy enough to handle, I should think."

"I suppose you're both right," Trixie sighed, "but. . . ."

"But what?" Brian laughed.

"It's just that I have a feeling, that's all."

Mart groaned, and Brian sighed and rolled his eyes ceilingward.

"You know, her feelings have been right before," Honey said, in Trixie's defense.

"I know," Brian admitted, "but don't you think that Miss Darcy has enough on her mind without Trixie bothering her with some crazy notion about costumes?"

"Okay, okay! Time out. I get the message." Trixie grinned good-naturedly. "I'd better get downstairs and start wooing Bobby with stories, or he'll never go to bed. He's so excited about Reddy coming home tomorrow."

"I'll read to him for a while," Honey offered, following Trixie down the stairs. Brian and Mart went to their rooms to finish their homework.

"You weren't listening to anything they said, were you?" Honey whispered.

"Not a word!" Trixie laughed. "In fact, my hunches are getting hunchier—if that's a word. I've *got* to get another look at those costumes—and that catalog!"

Curious Costumes and Catalogs • 7

THE NEXT MORNING, Trixie and Honey awoke to the smell of frying bacon. "I don't think there's a more wonderful aroma in the world," Trixie sighed, rolling over and sitting up. "It's that kind of warm, get-up-and-get-going smell."

"And that's exactly what we've got to do—get up and get going." Honey yawned and stretched.

The two girls dressed quickly and hurried down to the breakfast table.

"What a feast!" Mart exclaimed, eyeing the big stack of golden brown pancakes and the platter of crisp bacon. "This is usually Sunday-morning-breakfast fare. I think Honey should stay over more often, if it means weekday breakfasts like this." He sat down and quickly filled his plate.

"I thought I'd make something special this morning," Mrs. Belden said. "Since you're driving to school today, there's no rush to make the bus, and besides, we have a guest."

"Thank you, Mrs. Belden," Honey said.

"And such a *polite* guest, at that," Helen Belden added, clearing her throat.

"Oops! Yeah, Moms, thank you," Trixie said. Brian and Mart added their thanks, too.

Brian finished eating first, so he went to pick up Jim and Di. He had called them the night before and offered them a ride to school.

"I'll swing by and pick all of you up in about fifteen minutes, so no third helpings this morning, Mart," Brian warned.

"I'm so 'cited about Reddy coming home, I can hardly eat any potcakes," Bobby said.

"Potcakes?" Honey chuckled. "You mean *pan*cakes."

"Oh, yeah," Bobby giggled.

Everyone had finished breakfast and was ready to go when Brian sounded the horn of the

Bob-White station wagon.

"I don't know if we'll be able to get everyone in the car for the ride home, with Reddy in here," Brian said as they started off down Glen Road. "Unless, of course, someone's willing to sit way in the back."

"No problem," Jim offered. "I'll crawl back there. Reddy should have a full-fledged Bob-White welcome-home party."

"Fine with me," Brian said. A short time later, he was pulling into the student parking lot at Sleepyside High. "Everyone meet here, then, right after school, and we'll go pick up Reddy."

Trixie ran to her locker, hung up her coat, and grabbed the books she needed for her first two classes. *I want to have a few minutes to talk to Miss Darcy when I return this envelope*, she thought, hurrying to the drama teacher's office.

At Trixie's gentle knock Miss Darcy opened the door. "Oh, Trixie, I've been waiting for you. Thank you for returning this envelope. Here's the right one." Eileen Darcy sighed with obvious relief.

"I thought it was important, so I—" Trixie began, but she was interrupted by the sound of the warning bell.

"You'd better go along to your class," Miss Darcy said as she put the envelope in her desk drawer.

Trixie quickly looked around the room, hoping to see the catalog that Peter Ashbury had caught her looking at the day before. She spotted it on top of a bookcase.

"Oh, Miss Darcy, do you mind if I borrow this?" she asked rapidly, reaching for the catalog. "Honey Wheeler is very interested in costume design, and I thought she might like to see it."

"Honey is welcome to come in here and look at it," Eileen Darcy said coolly. "I have a number of other costume books that would probably be more suitable."

"I'll tell her," Trixie said casually, and put the catalog back on the bookcase. Then she hurried out the door and down the hall to her first class.

There is something strange about that catalog—I just know it! Trixie thought. She turned things over and over again in her mind, trying to sort through them and find some explanation. *Of course, Brian and Mart could be right—it might be nothing. But I've got to get another look at that catalog! I wonder if. . . .*

That's it! Trixie's eyes widened with surprise at the thought that had just occurred to her.

She could hardly contain her excitement. As soon as it was time for rehearsal, Trixie raced to the auditorium, hoping Honey would already be there.

"Just as I thought," Trixie said aloud, scanning the auditorium.

"Just as you thought what?"

Trixie jumped. "Honey! You startled me. I was originally looking for you to tell you something important, but then something else occurred to me. I didn't even realize I'd said that out loud."

The other students were just beginning to enter the auditorium. Trixie pulled Honey to one side.

"Look who isn't here today," Trixie whispered intently.

"What do you mean? Who isn't here? Trixie, what are you talking about?"

"Peter Ashbury. He's always here at this time."

"Maybe he just couldn't make it today," Honey said.

"No," Trixie said slowly, "I don't think we're

going to be seeing him around here anymore—now that the costumes have arrived."

"What?" Honey asked, completely befuddled.

"Listen," Trixie went on excitedly, "suppose Miss Darcy needed money, a lot of money, like maybe for a ransom payment. If Ashbury works for a costume company, and those costumes are really valuable, and he knows *how* valuable, and he has the right contacts, he could sell them!"

"W-e-e-l-l-l," Honey began uncertainly, "I suppose you might be right. But I can't imagine that the costumes are that valuable, especially if Miss Darcy's friend is letting us use them. I also can't imagine Miss Darcy getting mixed up in something like that."

"That's true," Trixie said, somewhat crestfallen. "But we'll find that out soon enough," she added mysteriously.

Honey stared. "What do you mean?"

"First," Trixie began, but just then Miss Darcy entered the auditorium and called the class to order.

"Talk to you after rehearsal," Trixie whispered. Honey hurried to the wardrobe room, and Trixie took her place with the stagehands.

"We'll be trying on the costumes from England on Monday," Miss Darcy announced, and Trixie sighed with disappointment. "The wardrobe crew is working on the other costumes we will need," Miss Darcy continued, "and we will have fittings for all of them next week. Today the stagehands, under the guidance of Jim Frayne, will finish painting the remaining backdrops and begin collecting props."

As the drama teacher turned her attention to the cast, Trixie walked slowly to the wings and began setting up the painting supplies.

"What's wrong, Trixie?" Jim asked. "I thought you were so excited about everyone working together on this production. Are you losing interest?"

"Actually, Jim, my interest is somewhere else right now," Trixie responded absentmindedly.

"I've heard rumblings along those lines from Mart and Brian."

"What have they been saying?" Trixie demanded hotly.

"Now, now," Jim cautioned her. "You always blame my temper on my red hair. What am I going to blame yours on, those curls?"

111

Trixie blushed and ran her fingers through her hair self-consciously. "Oh, Jim, you know how they make fun of me," she cried, "and I know I'm right about this!"

"Don't underestimate them," Jim said gently. "They just don't want you getting too carried away. Besides, Trixie Belden, I have a bone to pick with you. Why didn't you let me in on any of your suspicions? I realize that I'm not part of the Belden-Wheeler detective team, but I certainly have an interest in what you're doing."

"It all happened so fast," Trixie said defensively, "and you know Honey and me when things start to happen."

"I know, I know," Jim laughed, "but just don't go taking a swan dive before you know how deep the water is, Trix."

Trixie smiled and said, "We'd better stop talking and start working. Everyone else is already hard at work, and you're supposed to be setting an example, Mr. Senior Aide," she added teasingly.

Jim laughed and went to help a group of freshmen work on one of the set designs.

As soon as class ended, Trixie ran to the costume room to meet Honey.

112

"Honey," she whispered as the other students filed past, "are the costumes from England with all the others?"

"No," Honey answered. "I don't know where they are. I haven't seen them since Miss Darcy opened the boxes in the auditorium yesterday."

"Hmmmmm," Trixie said. "Okay. Come with me."

"I hope we're going to the cafeteria. I'm famished, and it's lunchtime," Honey said as she followed Trixie down the hall.

"I'm hungry, too, but we've got to do some sleuthing first. We're going to take a look at that catalog."

"Trixie!" Honey cried. "We can't just walk into Miss Darcy's office. What if she comes in, or Peter Ashbury shows up, or—or—anything?" she concluded in exasperation.

"No, no, Honey!" Trixie cried in dismay. "We're not going to sneak into Miss Darcy's office! She'll be right there! I've already got an excuse for going to see her," Trixie explained. "I asked Miss Darcy if you could look at the catalog. I told her you were very interested in costume design."

Honey sighed and gave Trixie a dubious look.

"Don't look at me like that, Honey," Trixie said desperately. "I thought we were a team. Don't you want to solve this mystery?"

"You know I do, Trixie, and you know I think you're terrifically smart about clues, and I trust your feelings, but. . . ."

"But what?" Trixie asked cautiously.

"Well, this time I don't know," Honey replied uncomfortably. "There doesn't seem to be that much to go on, and Miss Darcy is a friend of Miss Trask's, and the more I've thought about it— Well, couldn't we just go to Miss Trask and ask her to talk to Miss Darcy? I'm sure she wouldn't tell *us* if something were wrong, but she might tell Miss Trask."

Trixie's face was set with firm determination. She looked directly at Honey.

"Honey Wheeler, I haven't heard such squeamishness from you since we found the diamond ring on the floor of the gatehouse and you kept wanting to turn it over to the police."

"I know," Honey sighed. "But it just seems kind of hard to believe that someone as nice as Miss Darcy and someone as handsome as Peter Ashbury—"

Trixie hooted. "So *that's* it! What's that line

from *Romeo and Juliet*: 'What's in a name?' Well, what's in a *face*, Honey? Good-looking people can be involved in crime just as easily as anyone else, and so can 'nice' people."

"I know that. I just mean—well, if someone looks so nice, how could they . . . ? You know what I mean," Honey finished miserably.

"I know," Trixie reassured her. "But we're wasting time. If we want to get to the drama office and still have time to eat lunch, we'd better hurry. All you have to do is to keep talking to Miss Darcy about costume design while we look through the catalog. I also want to get a look at the prices of some of those costumes."

"Okay," Honey answered nervously.

"And don't be afraid," Trixie reassured her. "We aren't doing anything wrong. We're just being—" she stopped, searching for the right words—"interested students."

They arrived at the drama club office and knocked. "Come in," Miss Darcy called.

"Hi," Trixie said casually, poking her head in the door. "I told Honey about the costume catalog, and she was anxious to see it. We had a few minutes, so we thought we'd stop in."

Eileen Darcy looked at them curiously. "Of

course," she said. "Please come in. Here is one on eighteenth-century costumes." Miss Darcy selected a book from the shelf and handed it to Honey. "And here's another one on Early Am—"

"Where is the catalog?" Trixie interrupted. Then she stopped, regretting that she had spoken so quickly.

"The catalog?" Eileen Darcy asked.

"I—I didn't mean to interrupt," Trixie stammered. "It was the one with all the beautiful Shakespearean costumes. I saw it on top of the bookcase this morning."

"I'd rather not lend that one to you right now," Miss Darcy said coldly. "Now, if you'll excuse me, I have only a few minutes to eat my lunch before rehearsal time. If you'd like to borrow these two books for now, next week you can stop in after class someday and look at the Shakespearean catalog." Her tone was firm, dismissing them.

"We're sorry to bother you," Trixie apologized. "I know you must be worried about your father. Has there been any news yet?"

Eileen Darcy turned pale and began rearranging some papers on her desk.

"No, nothing yet," she said quietly.

"I'm sorry to hear that," Trixie said.

"So am I," Honey added. "I guess we'd better be going. Thank you for lending me these books." She gave Trixie a gentle nudge.

Trixie thanked Eileen Darcy, too, and the two girls left the office.

"Why did you start asking her about her father?" Honey whispered as they hurried toward the cafeteria.

Trixie looked at her friend in surprise. "Don't you see? There *is* something about that catalog. Didn't you notice how nervous she was when I asked about it? And how she changed the subject? I was kind of testing her to see how she'd react if I mentioned her father right after we talked about the catalog. You see, if—"

"Trixie!" Honey exclaimed. "You really do *plot*, don't you? I mean, I never would have thought of that!"

Trixie laughed. "Sometimes you have to *make* clues, not just stumble on them the way we usually do. I'm disappointed, though, that she wouldn't let us see the catalog. We've just got to get a look at it. I have another lead to track down, too. I want to talk to Bill Morgan."

"Why?" Honey asked. "I'd rather stay clear of the Morgan family altogether."

"I want to know more about those pictures Peter Ashbury wanted copies of," Trixie replied, "*and* I'd like to get a look at the costumes again. If those pictures have been developed. . . . In fact," Trixie mused, "I think I'll run up to the newspaper office right now. Why don't you go on ahead to the cafeteria and eat? I'll be there in a few minutes."

Before Honey could open her mouth to protest, Trixie had turned and was hurrying down the hall.

She ran up two steps at a time to the third floor of the school building, and arrived at the door of the *Campus Clarion* offices. The door was open, so she poked her head in.

"Hi!" she said to the blond girl sitting at one of the editorial desks. "Is Bill Morgan around?"

"He was just here," the girl answered. "He said he had an errand to do but he'd be right back."

"Mind if I wait a few minutes?" Trixie asked.

"No, sit down." The girl smiled pleasantly. "I'm Monica Anderson. You're Trixie Belden, aren't you?"

"Yes," Trixie answered. "I'm surprised—"

"Don't be," Monica interrupted. "Lots of kids in this school know about your detective work. You've become something of a celebrity, actually." Monica laughed as Trixie blushed. "Don't be embarrassed," she said. "I'm a big mystery fan myself. I read every detective story I can get my hands on. Are you working on a case now?" she asked, leaning across the desk eagerly.

"I wish I knew," Trixie sighed.

Just then, much to Trixie's relief, Bill Morgan walked into the office. She jumped up to greet him. He was a tall, good-looking boy with sandy-colored hair and pale green eyes.

"Hi, Bill," Trixie said, smiling. "I'm Trixie Belden."

"Oh, yeah!" He smiled back. "I've heard my kid sister talk about you."

I'm sure you have, Trixie thought grimly.

Monica got up from her desk. "I've got to run," she said. "See you later, Bill. It was nice meeting you, Trixie."

As Monica left, Trixie breathed a soft sigh of relief. She didn't want to talk to Bill in front of her, especially since she was a mystery fan.

"So what can I do for you, Trixie Belden?"

119

Bill Morgan asked jovially. "If you want to work on the paper, I'm sorry, but freshmen—"

"Oh, no," Trixie assured him. "I only came to ask you about some pictures you took of the costumes for the freshman class play."

Bill eyed her suspiciously. "You're the second person who's asked me about those pictures."

"Oh?" Trixie asked innocently.

"Yeah. The drama teacher's boyfriend, Mr. Ashbury, wanted some copies of them. He offered to pay me a good price for them, too. But now—" Bill stopped and looked at Trixie again. "Why do you want them, anyway?"

"Actually," Trixie began, groping frantically for an excuse, "my friend Di Lynch is playing Juliet, and I wanted to put together a kind of scrapbook of the play for her as a surprise. You know—" Trixie paused. "I thought the pictures would be a nice thing to add."

"Yeah, well, sorry I can't help you out." Bill shrugged.

"Why not?" Trixie asked.

"I can't exactly give you copies of pictures I don't have," Bill snapped.

"What do you mean, you don't have them?"

"The film is gone—poof!" he cried, gesturing

like a magician doing a disappearing act. "I thought I had left it in the camera, but when I came back here to develop it after school yesterday, it was gone. I've looked everywhere, and I've asked everyone who works on the paper, but it hasn't turned up yet. I guess both you and Mr. Ashbury are out of luck—until I take some more pictures, that is, and Miss Darcy won't let me do that until next week."

"She won't?" Trixie asked, trying hard to contain her excitement.

"Nope." Bill shrugged. "I didn't ask why, but it's really not important. The *Gazette* doesn't want the article for a couple of weeks yet, anyway. I was just going to write to Mr. Ashbury and tell him the film had been lost."

"Did he say why he wanted the pictures?" Trixie asked, as casually as she could.

"No." Bill shook his head. "You know, you certainly ask a lot of questions."

"Just curious," Trixie laughed lightly. "Well, I'd better run. I have to eat before rehearsal." She left quickly, before Bill could become even more suspicious of her curiosity.

Trixie's head was spinning as she walked down the stairs toward the cafeteria. *I'll bet*

121

that film isn't lost, she thought excitedly. *I'll bet someone took it, and that someone could very well be Peter Ashbury!* She wished she had asked for Ashbury's address, but she hadn't dared—Bill Morgan had been getting too suspicious as it was. *I think I need a shift chart for this case*, she giggled to herself.

Trixie glanced at her watch and realized that it was time for rehearsal and she hadn't eaten her lunch yet. She hurried to the auditorium. It seemed that all she'd been doing that day was rushing from one place to the next. *And now my stomach will be growling all afternoon, like Reddy when he sees a jackrabbit!* She groaned at the thought.

But the afternoon flew by, and Trixie didn't again think about missing lunch, until she met the rest of the Bob-Whites after school.

"Boy, am I famished!" she cried, climbing into the backseat of the station wagon. "I hope my lunch is still fresh."

"That sounds like a typical Mart greeting," Brian said, "but it has a definitely higher pitch. Where were you at lunch today, Trixie?"

"I had some things to do." Trixie shrugged as she unwrapped a sandwich and eagerly took a bite. "You know," she said between mouthfuls, "I'll never understand how Moms gets this waxed paper to work right. It's always been a complete mystery to me."

Mart hooted. "Was everyone witness to that statement? Trixie admits that something is a complete mystery to her. How about this for your next case, Sherlock: 'The Puzzling Predicament of Paraffined Paper'?"

"Mart, how does waxed paper get into a predicament?" Trixie asked, still laughing as Di got into the car.

"Sorry I'm late," Di apologized, "but I forgot my script, and I had to run back and get it."

"How are rehearsals going?" Brian asked.

Di groaned. "Only five weeks left, and there's still so much to do! I'm never quite sure if I'm supposed to enter stage left and exit stage right—or versa vice—from one scene to the next."

"I can understand why," Jim chuckled, "especially since it's *vice versa*."

"See?" Di wailed. "That's another problem. I keep getting my words mixed up."

"Don't worry," Honey reassured her. "I've been watching you, and you're doing fine. In another few weeks, you'll be ready for Broadway—or Hollywood."

"No, thanks!" Di cried. "I'll settle for just being ready for the stage at Sleepyside High."

Brian had maneuvered the car out of the parking lot and was headed toward the veterinarian's office. "I can hardly wait to see Bobby's face when we bring Reddy home," he said.

"We've all been anxious to get him back," Trixie added. "I've missed that crazy dog."

Honey, who was sitting next to Trixie, nudged her gently in the side. She was dying to know what Trixie had found out from Bill Morgan about the pictures. Trixie gave Honey an I-can't-wait-to-talk-to-you-either look as Brian pulled into Dr. Samet's driveway.

Brian, Trixie, and Mart got out of the car. The old veterinarian met them at the doorway. "Come in, come in," he said. "I have one very anxious Irish setter here who will be very glad to see you three."

Dr. Samet was right. As the Belden trio entered the room, Reddy gave a happy bark, and as fast as he could with the cast still on his front leg, he hobbled over and gave them each a slurpy kiss as they bent down to hug him.

"Old Reddy certainly has a mind of his own," Dr. Samet chuckled as he gave the Irish setter a playful rub on the neck.

"*That* is the understatement of the year," Mart said. "He's totally untrainable for anything, I'm afraid."

"A true free spirit," Dr. Samet agreed.

"Well, I think he behaves terribly!" a voice from the other side of the room interjected.

"Jane!" the veterinarian exclaimed.

Trixie, Brian, and Mart turned to meet Jane's cool gaze.

"Well, he does," she went on, "and I think it's disgraceful when people don't train their pets properly."

Trixie felt the heat of outrage as her cheeks flushed a bright scarlet. She wanted to say something, but the anger seemed to bottle up her words, and she could only stare at Jane in shocked disbelief.

"He is well fed and well treated, Jane," Dr. Samet said firmly. "It is not necessary to train a dog to sit and retrieve. It is only necessary to love him, and Reddy certainly gets plenty of affection. You owe the Beldens an apology; there was no need for such rudeness."

125

It was Jane's turn to feel uncomfortable, and she glanced guiltily at her uncle. "Sorry, Uncle David. I didn't mean to sound so harsh, and . . . and I'm sorry I was rude," she added quickly to the three Beldens. Then she turned and left the room.

Dr. Samet turned to face the trio, a deep furrow creasing his brow. "I don't know what's wrong with her lately," he apologized. "She's usually so good with the animals—and with their owners. She's been talking about going to vet school—Jane's very good in math and science—" He rambled on for several more minutes, obviously troubled by his niece's outburst. "I'm sorry. I'm keeping you," he said finally, "and I apologize again for Jane's behavior."

"That's okay." Trixie shrugged, although she was still seething. "Actually, when you said 'math and science,' it reminded me that I have an algebra quiz on Monday morning, and I forgot my book."

"As you can see," Mart volunteered, "Reddy isn't the only irresponsible member of the Belden household."

"Well, we'd better swing by school and pick up your book," Brian sighed. He thanked Dr.

Sam et for all his help, then gently picked Reddy up in his arms.

Trixie and Mart added their thanks as they helped Brian get Reddy out the door and down the front steps.

"What took so long?" Jim asked as they all repositioned themselves to make room for the disabled Irish setter.

"You wouldn't believe it!" Trixie finally exploded as she related the encounter with Jane to Jim, Honey, and Di.

"I don't know what kind of bee she has in her bonnet," Jim said, "but whatever it is, it has a very nasty sting sometimes."

"Do you have some kind of beef with her, Trix?" Mart asked.

"Not that I know of," Trixie said hotly, "but I've had just about enough of her."

"It's because she's so jealous," Honey explained quietly.

"I know," Di added quietly. "She wanted the part of Juliet so badly. She even came to me and asked me to quit the play."

"She *did?*" Trixie exclaimed in wide-eyed amazement. "And here Honey and I have been keeping quiet about what she's been saying!"

Di sighed again. "I—I didn't want to tell you," she went on, a catch in her voice, "because I was afraid that you all agreed with what she thought—that she could play the role much better than I could."

"Don't be ridiculous!" Trixie exclaimed.

"Oh, Di," Honey said sympathetically, "of *course* we don't think that."

"Why are we going back toward town?" Jim asked suddenly, realizing that Brian was not headed for home.

"Because our scatterbrained sibling neglected to bring one of her textbooks home," Mart explained teasingly, hoping to break some of the tension the discussion about Jane had created.

"Gleeps!" Trixie cried. "I forgot about it again! If you hadn't remembered to come back, Brian. . . ."

"I don't think you are fully cognizant of the fact that you are truly blessed, Beatrix," Mart said. "Without the assistance of your two highly responsible elder brothers, I'm afraid you would be totally incapable of—"

"All right, all right." Trixie sighed in exasperation. "I can't help it I get sidetracked sometimes."

"Sidetracked!" Mart hooted. "I didn't think that muddled mass of gray matter *had* more than one track, Miss Belden."

Brian pulled up in front of the school. Trixie made a face at Mart, then hopped out of the car and ran up the front steps of the building. Fortunately, the doors were still open.

Trixie hurried down the hall to her locker and quickly found the necessary book. *I don't know why I even bother trying to study this*, she thought as she headed back toward the exit.

As she passed the drama club office, she noticed a thin stream of light spilling into the darkened hallway. *Miss Darcy must be working late*, Trixie thought. *I should stop and tell her that we just picked up Reddy*. She knocked softly and peeked around the edge of the partly open door.

Eileen Darcy looked up quickly and started in surprise. She dropped something from her hand, and it fell to the floor, catching the light in sparkling silvery rays.

"I—I didn't mean to scare you," Trixie stammered, her eyes on the shiny stone lying at her feet. She bent down to retrieve it. Eileen Darcy jumped up from her chair, lunged for the stone, and snatched it from Trixie's fingers. The costume she'd been holding in her lap fell limply to the floor.

"Don't you knock before bursting in on someone?" the drama teacher demanded as she picked up the costume.

"I—I did knock," Trixie answered timidly, and went on to explain why she had stopped.

Miss Darcy's tone softened slightly after hearing Trixie's explanation. "I'm sorry. I was just very startled," she said, nervously smoothing out the wrinkled skirt of the velvet gown she held in her hands. "I was working late, resewing and securing some of the decorations on these lovely costumes. They were loose—it must have happened during shipping."

Trixie nodded, but her eyes wandered to the desk top, where a small pile of bright gems and a pair of scissors lay. Miss Darcy caught her look. Dropping the dress on the chair, she took Trixie by the arm and steered her firmly toward the door.

"Thank you for letting me know about Reddy," Eileen Darcy said rapidly. "I'll walk you to the entrance." They left the office and headed down the corridor. At the large glass doors,

Miss Darcy waved a quick good-bye, then turned and hurried back toward her office.

In the car, the rest of the Bob-Whites were chatting and laughing and playing with Reddy. Trixie joined in the fun, not wanting to explain what had just happened until she'd had time to think about it.

Brian took Di home, then headed east on Glen Road toward Manor House.

"Why don't you drop us off at the end of our drive?" Jim suggested. "I know you're anxious to get Reddy home."

"Okay," Brian agreed. "Thanks."

The Beldens waved good-bye to their friends as they headed for Crabapple Farm.

Bobby must have been waiting at the back door, for as the station wagon crunched to a halt on the gravel driveway, he came flying out, flung open the car door, and threw his arms around Reddy's neck.

Trixie, Brian, and Mart got out of the car and stood watching the confused scene. Reddy was wriggling from head to tail and trying to cover every inch of Bobby with his sloppy kisses. Bobby was giggling and crying and trying to hug Reddy, all at the same time.

Though her eyes were moist, Trixie burst into laughter and dove into the tangle to hug her brother and the frantic dog.

"Hey, Trixie," Bobby gulped happily. "Reddy's not mad at me!"

"Of course not, honey," Trixie laughed, fending off the exuberant dog. "He loves you!"

Somehow, the three older Beldens untangled the boy and the dog, and Brian carried Reddy inside to his waiting bed.

Dinner that evening was a hectic affair, but no one minded. It was far past his bedtime when Bobby finally settled down enough to fall asleep.

Trixie fell into bed, exhausted by the events of the day. She lay awake for some time, however, going over the encounter with Miss Darcy in the drama club office. Her thoughts became more and more confused, until finally she decided to stop trying to figure things out.

I do know one thing, though, Trixie thought grimly. *I don't know* why, *but I do know that Miss Darcy wasn't sewing those decorations onto the costumes—she was cutting them* off!

New York City Adventure • 8

HELEN BELDEN gently shook her daughter's shoulder, rousing her out of a deep sleep. "Trixie," she said.

"Wh-what?" Trixie asked, bleary-eyed and confused. "Moms, isn't it Saturday?" she mumbled, glancing at the bedside clock.

"Yes, dear, but Miss Trask just called. Her sister in New York City came down with a stomach virus yesterday, and Miss Trask is going to take the eight-thirty train in to do some errands and laundry for her. She asked if you would like to go along with them. Apparently,

Honey has asked to go along."

Trixie was suddenly wide awake. "Boy, *would* I! But, Moms," Trixie sighed, looking somewhat sheepish, "what about. . . ."

"The chores," her mother finished for her. "Miss Trask said she plans to catch the two o'clock train back this afternoon, so you'll have time to finish whatever I don't get done today. I'll help you out—just this once." Mrs. Belden smiled.

"Moms, you're terrific!" Trixie cried, giving her mother a quick hug. "I must be the luckiest girl in the world."

Mrs. Belden laughed. "I don't know about the luckiest, but you certainly are one of the most active. Now, hurry up and get dressed. They're going to stop on their way to the train station to pick you up."

Trixie hurriedly pulled on a pair of blue wool pants and a sweater. *I can't believe it*, she thought. *What luck!*

She and Honey had spent an hour on the phone the night before, which had brought a scolding from Peter Belden about tying up the phone lines. "But," Trixie had wailed, "it was so important, I just *had* to talk to her!"

"Of course you did," Mart had teased. "Nobody could walk around with as many secrets and important things to discuss as you do. You had to tell someone before you burst. Fortunately, Honey will listen to you. It saves us, at least."

Trixie had almost taken the bait, but then she'd thought twice about it and had laughed it off. *Mart is already watching me too closely*, she'd warned herself. *I'd better play it cool for a while, at least until I have some more evidence.*

She'd told Honey everything she'd learned from Bill Morgan about the pictures, and she'd admitted that while she suspected Peter Ashbury of stealing the film, she hadn't yet figured out why or how. She had related the whole incident with Miss Darcy after school.

"See, Honey?" she had said. "There is something strange about Peter Ashbury and those costumes and Miss Darcy, if only we could figure out what the link is."

Honey had been puzzled by everything, too, and had said, quite offhandedly, "If only we could tail Mr. Ashbury for a while. . . ."

Trixie had been secretly pleased that Honey would ever suggest anything so daring. "Now you're talking," Trixie had told her. "I was getting worried about your lack of enthusiasm for this mystery."

Quickly running a brush through her sandy curls, Trixie smiled at her reflection as she recalled Honey's surprising suggestion. Now, as if by magic, they had the perfect chance. *If only*—she thought—*if only we can find out exactly where Peter Ashbury works.*

Trixie was so excited at the prospect of a day's sleuthing that she bounded down the stairs and burst into the kitchen, only to be reminded by her mother that other members of the family were still asleep.

"Gleeps!" Trixie cried, putting her hand over her mouth. "Sorry, Moms. I got so carried away, I forgot," she added in a whisper.

"Well, you'd better have a quick, *quiet* bowl of cereal—nothing that snaps, gargles, or roars, please. They'll be here any minute."

"I'm too excited to eat," Trixie said.

"My goodness," Mrs. Belden laughed, "you're acting as if you'd never been to the city before."

"It's like a little surprise vacation, that's all," Trixie said, pulling on her coat. "I'll walk to the end of the driveway to meet them." She gave her mother a good-bye kiss. "Thanks for letting me off the hook with chores, Moms."

"Have a good time." Helen Belden smiled and closed the door behind her daughter. She watched from the kitchen window as Trixie jogged to the end of the driveway.

Miss Trask soon pulled up in the Wheelers' sedan and stopped alongside the entrance to the Beldens' drive. Trixie had been waiting eagerly, hopping on one foot and then the other, trying to keep warm in the frosty morning air.

"Hi," she said, climbing into the backseat.

"Sorry we woke you and your mother up so early this morning, Trixie," Honey said, giving her friend a knowing, sidelong glance, "but I thought it would be fun to keep Miss Trask company on the train ride."

"Oh," Trixie said, remembering the real reason for the trip. She turned to Miss Trask. "I was sorry to hear that your sister is sick. How is she?"

"It's just a stomach flu, nothing serious," Miss Trask replied. "But she needs to have a prescription filled and some laundry done. It's a little harder for her to manage with the wheelchair when she's ill, so I thought I would offer

137

to come in for a few hours." Miss Trask's sister had been an invalid for some time, but she was now able to live independently.

"Do you want us to help, too?" Honey asked. Trixie crossed her fingers and hoped that Miss Trask would say no, even though she knew that Honey had been right to offer to help.

"Goodness, no," Miss Trask answered. "I thought I'd drop you two off at the Metropolitan Museum of Art. It's only a few blocks from my sister's apartment, and there are quite a few interesting exhibits there now."

"Okay," Honey and Trixie agreed in unison.

They arrived at the Sleepyside station just in time to catch the eight-thirty train.

Miss Trask sighed with relief as they took their seats in the coach. "I'm glad we made this train. The next one doesn't leave for another hour. Trains don't run as frequently on the weekends as they do during the week, when all the commuters are going to work." Di's father was one of those commuters who made the hour-long train trip to and from New York City every day.

Honey and Trixie settled into a double seat across the aisle from Miss Trask as the train moved slowly away from the station. Soon Miss Trask was absorbed in a magazine. The humming rhythm of the train masked the whispering excitement Honey and Trixie shared.

"I can't believe it!" Trixie giggled. "Perfect timing."

"I know," Honey beamed. "When Miss Trask's sister called this morning, I couldn't help thinking, 'How did Trixie arrange *this*!' "

Trixie laughed, too, and then they settled back to watch out the window as the countryside slipped away and the skyline became crowded with buildings.

"The train seems to sound different when we get close to the city," Honey said, "as if it's getting more energy or something. In Sleepyside, it sounds like *chugga-chugga*, *chugga-chugga*, but now it sounds like *hustle-bustle*, *hustle-bustle*."

Trixie turned to Honey and laughed. "Have you ever thought about getting a job as a train engineer? I never knew you could do such a good train imitation, Honey. Do you do bird calls, too?"

Honey giggled. "You know what I mean," she said. "The train does sound different."

"I think so, too," Trixie said. "I was just laughing about your 'hustle-bustle, hustle-bustle.' It sounds like a new dance step or something."

Just then the train dipped into the underground tunnel that led to the tracks of Grand Central Station. They were enveloped in darkness for several seconds until the train lights winked on.

"I always like this part of the trip best," Trixie said. "It's like going into some secret cave."

"Some secret!" Honey exclaimed. "When you come out, you find yourself in one of the world's busiest train stations."

Trixie laughed. "Now I guess it's my turn to say 'You know what I mean. . . .' "

The conductor's voice came over the loudspeaker to inform everyone that this was the last stop on the line.

Honey and Trixie gathered up their coats and followed Miss Trask off the train. They walked through the underground network of hallways and waiting rooms until they arrived at the center of the beautiful old terminal.

"Look up," Miss Trask said. She pointed, directing their attention to the huge barrel-vaulted ceiling of the concourse. Ornate arches bordered the blue-tiled ceiling, which was studded with small, starlike lights. The lights twinkled along the gold outlines that depicted the mythical characters of the zodiac.

"It's lovely," Honey whispered.

"You know, I never looked up in this station before," Trixie admitted. "I was always so busy trying not to bump into anyone or looking for the information booth or something that I never even thought of it."

"Neither did I," Honey confessed. "Look! There's Pegasus." Her pointing finger followed the outline of the head and shoulders of the winged horse.

"Fine detectives you'll make," Miss Trask sniffed teasingly. "You've got to look up, down, and all around."

Honey and Trixie giggled. "You're absolutely right, though!" Trixie added emphatically.

When they reached the street, Miss Trask hailed a cab and directed the driver to the Metropolitan Museum of Art.

"I'll drop you off there and go on to my sister's," Miss Trask explained. "It's almost ten o'clock now. I'll be back at noon, and we'll all

141

go somewhere for lunch before catching the two o'clock train back to Sleepyside. You kids should be able to keep yourselves busy for two hours. I'll meet you at the front entrance."

Honey and Trixie nodded in agreement, and shortly, the cab stopped in front of the museum. The two girls got out of the cab and waved good-bye to Miss Trask.

"We've got a lot of work to do in two hours," Trixie said as she and Honey began the long climb up the steps to the museum entrance. "They should have a phone book somewhere here," she added.

"Uh-huh." Honey giggled. "It might be an antique, but it *will* be a phone book."

"This building really is beautiful," Trixie panted as they neared the huge glass-doored entrance, "but I don't see why they couldn't have made fewer steps."

With careful directions from a museum guard, the two girls went to find a telephone. "You really could get lost in this place, it's so big," Honey said.

Trixie agreed. "In fact," she added, pointing to the Egyptian exhibit as they passed, "those really aren't mummies, you know. Those are people who never found their way out of this place, and the museum decided to keep them."

"Oooh, wouldn't it be terrible if that were so?" Honey shuddered slightly and hurried past the rest of the mummy exhibit.

They soon found the phone book, and Trixie quickly looked up *Ashbury, Peter*. "Here it is!" she cried excitedly. "I was afraid he might have an unlisted number, but he doesn't. I only hope this is the Peter Ashbury we're looking for," she added, jotting down the address.

"Now let's hope our luck holds out and this address isn't on the other side of town," Trixie said, heading toward another museum guard to ask directions.

"That's only two blocks from here," the guard assured them, and he went on to explain exactly how to get there.

"We certainly are lucky today," Honey said happily. "Maybe one of the 'stars' we stood under in the station was lucky."

"I sure hope so," Trixie sighed, "but remember, we have to look up, down, and all around as Miss Trask said. We can't always count on luck to find clues. And," Trixie added, "we'd better make sure our watches are right. We

TRIXIE BELDEN

can't exactly be running *up* the stairs of the museum at noon, when Miss Trask will be expecting to see us come *down* them."

Honey's face clouded slightly, and she frowned. "I do feel guilty about deceiving Miss Trask. She's so terrific and she trusts us. . . ."

"I feel guilty, too," Trixie admitted, "but you know if we asked permission to follow Peter Ashbury, the fiancé of a friend of hers, because we suspected he was a criminal, she wouldn't exactly smile and say, 'Go ahead.' "

"I know," Honey sighed, "but I just feel . . . well, you know. I'm already worried that we'll have to tell her something about the exhibits we saw."

"Gleeps, you're right!" Trixie exclaimed. "We'd better be back here at eleven-thirty so we have time to take a quick look at *some*thing."

Honey agreed as they reached the bottom of the long flight of steps and were on the street again.

"Now, we just have to walk east two blocks," Trixie said, recalling the guard's directions.

As the girls crossed Fifth Avenue, Honey pointed out the Empire State Building.

"This really is an exciting city," Trixie said,

144

"but I don't think I could take the *hustle-bustle, hustle-bustle* all the time."

"I know what you mean," Honey said seriously. She and her parents had lived in an apartment in New York before moving to Sleepyside. Then she laughed. "And besides, where would the horses get their exercise? Can you imagine Jupe, with all his wild energy, pulling one of those hansom cabs?" she asked. Jupiter—or Jupe, for short—was a large black gelding, one of the five horses in the Wheelers' stable.

"I certainly can't," Trixie laughed. "The passengers would be in for a wild ride through Central Park with Jupe in the lead."

Trixie stopped and pointed to a blue canopy with the numbers 268 emblazoned on the side. "That's the address," she said. "Come on!" The two girls hurried into the beautiful old apartment building and were met at the entrance by a neatly uniformed doorman.

"May I help you, young ladies?" he asked in a formal tone.

"I hope so." Trixie smiled. "Does a Mr. Peter Ashbury live here?"

"Yes, he does, miss. Would you like me to

ring him?" he asked, heading for the house phone.

"No, thank you," Trixie said hurriedly. "I—I wanted to send him something, and I just needed to make sure I had the correct address."

The doorman looked puzzled, but he just shrugged his shoulders.

"One more thing," Trixie said hastily. "Could you please tell me—is Mr. Ashbury a costume dealer?"

"Oh, no," the doorman answered. "He's—"

Just then, one of the elevator doors slid open, and Peter Ashbury stepped out. Trixie slipped her arm through Honey's, spun her around, and walked briskly through the revolving door. The doorman looked on, dumbfounded.

"Run!" Trixie hissed, and the two girls raced to the corner.

"What's going on?" Honey demanded, gasping for breath as they turned the corner and stopped.

Trixie glanced around the corner anxiously. "That was Peter Ashbury getting out of the elevator. I hope he didn't see us," she said worriedly. "I wish we'd had time to hear what the doorman had to say about Mr. Ashbury, but we can't exactly go back and ask him now. At least we know he's not a costume dealer."

Honey sighed. "Sorry I was wrong about that, but I still think I've seen him before."

Trixie kept poking her head around the corner, checking to see if Peter Ashbury had left the apartment building. Finally he appeared, neatly dressed in a tweed overcoat. A woman and two small children were with him.

"Good," Trixie said. "They're going the other way. Now we can follow them at a safe distance. Let's walk on the other side of the street, though, to avoid seeing that doorman again. I hope he didn't tell Mr. Ashbury that two girls were asking about him."

Honey shot Trixie a worried glance.

"Stop looking as if I'm making you walk the plank," Trixie said impatiently.

"Oh, Trixie," Honey said forlornly, "I'm not worried about following Peter Ashbury. But who are the woman and children with him?"

"I don't know," Trixie said, "but—"

"I think you're thinking the same thing I'm thinking. Poor Miss Darcy."

"We'd better be quiet and concentrate on following him. I don't want to lose him."

147

The two girls crossed the street, all the while keeping an eye on Peter Ashbury.

"He's turning down Madison Avenue," Trixie said. "Let's wait until he turns the corner."

Honey and Trixie continued to follow the group at a safe distance. Peter Ashbury and the woman strolled casually, occasionally glancing into store windows or holding up one of the children to point out something interesting in a display. At one point, Trixie feared that Peter Ashbury had seen them, and she and Honey dropped farther back, slowing their pace and speaking only occasionally.

Finally, at an intersection, Ashbury whirled around and looked straight at Trixie. He leaned over and said something to the woman, then turned and stalked angrily toward the two girls, a scowl disfiguring his handsome face.

Honey's first impulse was to run, but Trixie had gripped her arm and was holding it tightly. "Smile!" Trixie hissed under her breath as Peter Ashbury approached them.

"Hello, Mr. Ashbury." Trixie smiled with more confidence than she felt.

"So it *is* you!" he snapped. "What do you think you're doing, following me?"

"W-We're not following you!" Trixie stammered, her courage fading in the face of his anger. "We were—we were just window shopping. . . ." Her voice trailed off uncertainly.

Trixie's response seemed to confuse Ashbury, and he hesitated. *He's beginning to believe me*, she thought with relief. *He must not have seen us at his apartment building*.

Just then, Honey spoke up. "Yes, Mr. Ashbury," she said, affecting a slightly puzzled tone. "We thought it seemed like too nice a day to spend in a museum, so here we are. We were just wondering if that was you." Honey glanced at the woman and children, then quickly looked back at Ashbury, her hazel eyes innocently wide.

Trixie silently applauded her friend's performance. She could see that Honey's words had convinced Peter Ashbury.

"Yes, it's turned into a nice sunny day," he said, a little too heartily. "Very pleasant, for January. My . . . sister and I thought it would be a good day to take her children for an outing. Well, well. Nice seeing you girls." Then he turned and hurried away.

"Whew!" Honey sighed and seemed to melt

under Trixie's still-firm grip on her arm. "I knew he was going to see us."

"You were great!" Trixie exclaimed enthusiastically. Then she frowned. "But do you suppose that really was his sis—"

"Trixie!" Honey cried in alarm, glancing at her watch. "It's almost eleven-thirty! We've got to get back to the museum."

The two girls quickly hailed a cab and were soon on their way.

"I didn't realize we'd walked so far," Trixie said, as the meter clicked off another ten cents on the fare. When they arrived, Honey hurriedly paid the cabbie, and the two girls bounded up the steps to the museum entrance.

The guard who had given them directions earlier that morning spotted them entering the door. "I've never seen two girls so anxious to get into this museum," he chuckled. "Everything in here has been around for a long, long time, young ladies. It won't disappear in the next few minutes. Take your time—enjoy!" He smiled.

Trixie and Honey laughed and slowed their pace slightly. The first display was of ancient musical instruments, and they walked briskly up and down the wide aisles.

"Okay." Trixie took a deep breath. "We've just had a music lesson. Do you think we should tackle seventeenth-century art in the ten minutes we have left?" she asked, glancing at the panel describing the next exhibit.

"This is ridiculous!" Honey wailed, but before she had a chance to protest, Trixie was dragging her by the coat sleeve past paintings by Rembrandt and Velázquez.

"Try to remember at least one of these paintings," Trixie said urgently. "We've got to have something to tell Miss Trask."

Exactly at noon, the girls hurried back to the museum entrance. Miss Trask, always punctual, was waiting there for them. She didn't seem to notice Honey's sheepish look when she enthusiastically asked the girls about what they had seen.

Trixie, sensing Honey's guilt, chattered on about how much they had enjoyed the museum, and then she asked Miss Trask about her sister.

"She's feeling a little better," Miss Trask answered. "I'll call her tonight to check and see how she's doing, but right now, I'm famished. How would you two feel about one of those big hot dogs and some fries?"

"Miss Trask!" Honey exclaimed. "We'd love it, but it doesn't sound like the type of lunch you'd normally choose. It doesn't sound, well, sensible."

"Why not?" Miss Trask chuckled. "I enjoy a good hot dog just as much as the next person."

Honey laughed, too, and Trixie breathed a sigh of relief as she saw her friend relax and begin to forget about their sleuthing adventure, at least for the time being.

They made their way to the restaurant and leisurely enjoyed their lunch. They still had forty-five minutes left before their train, so they walked down Fifth Avenue, looking in the windows at Tiffany's and Cartier's.

"Look at that diamond," Honey said in awe. "It's immense! I bet Mother would love that."

"I don't understand why people buy so much expensive jewelry and then don't wear it," Trixie said. "They keep it locked up in safe-deposit boxes!"

Honey shrugged. "I suppose they consider it a good investment," she said. "My mother often wears her jewelry, though."

Miss Trask stopped at a newsstand just outside the station and bought a copy of *The New*

York Times. "Reading matter for the trip home," she said, neatly folding the paper and tucking it under her arm. "I left my magazines for my sister to read. We'd better get to our track," she said. "It's almost time for the two o'clock train. Sorry it had to be such a short day for you two. Next time we'll plan a whole day of shopping and sight-seeing."

Trixie cringed at the word *shopping*, one of her least favorite activities, but she nodded.

Miss Trask had caught her look, and she laughed. "I promise I won't drag you around, making you try on dresses. It will mostly be a day of sight-seeing."

As they arrived at the track, their train pulled in on the Hudson River line, and they boarded. The seats in the car they chose were all double and faced each other, like bookends placed back to back in a row. Miss Trask sat in one, and Honey and Trixie sat in the other, facing her.

Good, Trixie thought. *This is just what I need—some quiet time to piece all of this together.*

Miss Trask unfolded her paper and began to read, while Honey gazed dreamily out the train window, watching the buildings recede and finally disappear.

Suddenly Miss Trask gave a startled gasp, and her eyes widened as Honey and Trixie met her gaze.

"What is it?" Honey asked anxiously, leaning forward. Miss Trask's face had paled. "Do you feel all right?"

"It's . . . this article," Miss Trask answered slowly. "It's about Eileen Darcy's fiancé, Peter Ashbury. . . ."

More Pieces of the Puzzle • 9

"WHAT DOES IT SAY?" Trixie asked breathlessly.

"Look," Miss Trask answered shakily, and she handed the paper to Trixie.

Trixie's eyes widened as she read the article aloud to Honey:

"Peter Ashbury, the prominent gemologist who was dismissed from the prestigious Park Avenue Jewelers last month, will face a grand jury indictment early next week.

"Ashbury allegedly procured diamonds and other precious gems under the Park Avenue name, had paste imitations made, and sold the fake gems to Park Avenue customers, representing them as genuine. The fraud was discovered by one of the jewelry store's owners, B. Alfred Kelman.''

Trixie looked up from the page and saw her own shocked amazement reflected in Honey's eyes.

"Go *on*," Honey urged.

"When asked to comment on the allegations, Ashbury denied any involvement. 'They have no proof,' he claimed. 'What would I do with the real gems? Stones and settings from Park Avenue Jewelers would be recognized by other dealers.' "

I *know what he did with those gems!* Trixie thought fiercely as she continued to read. *Oh, poor Miss Darcy!*

"Kelman refuted Ashbury's statement, saying that the jewels could be easily removed from their original settings. 'Unfortunately,' Kelman added, 'there is a big market in this city for stolen gems.'

"The owners of Park Avenue Jewelers are contacting all customers who, within the last six months, have purchased jewelry set with precious gems, and are asking them to bring the stones in for evaluation.

" 'Ashbury was with us for six months,' Kelman said. 'He came to us with the highest recommendations, and a great many valuable stones have passed through his hands. We just hope that most of them were real.' "

Trixie finished reading and sat back in stunned silence.

Honey grabbed her arm excitedly. *"That's where I've seen him!"* she exclaimed. "Mother buys jewelry at that store, and I must have gone there with her at some time within the last six months!"

Trixie gaped at her. "You mean—Honey, your mother may have bought some fake jewels from them!"

Honey shook her head. "I doubt it. Mother can tell the difference between a real gem and a fake just by looking at them."

"Can you remember if she bought anything when you were with her?" Trixie asked.

"No, I can't, but we certainly have to tell her about this, if she hasn't already heard."

"Well, she certainly will be told," Miss Trask said to Honey. "Fortunately, your parents are returning from Miami tomorrow afternoon. Poor Eileen," she sighed, sinking back in her seat. "That young woman has had nothing but grief lately. First her father, then the accident, and now this."

"Do you think she knows about it?" Trixie asked anxiously.

"I don't know," Miss Trask reflected. "In fact, I don't ever remember her mentioning what Peter did for a living. She just always talked about how happy she was with him, until recently—" Miss Trask stopped, as if saying anything more would be breaking a confidence.

"I really don't know if she's aware of this," Miss Trask concluded simply. "She'll find out soon enough, I'm afraid." Then she turned her head and gazed out the train window, and the two girls knew she would say no more.

Honey and Trixie exchanged meaningful looks. Trixie's mind was whirling with this new information. *Gems, costumes, and catalogs! What does it all mean?* she puzzled as the train made its way toward Sleepyside-on-the-Hudson.

Nothing more was mentioned about Peter Ashbury or Eileen Darcy for the remainder of the trip, although Trixie was nearly bursting to share her deductions with Honey. She also wanted to ask Miss Trask more questions about Eileen Darcy, but she knew she'd get no answers.

The train finally pulled into the Sleepyside station. Miss Trask picked up the newspaper and once again tucked it neatly under her arm.

"Mrs. Wheeler will be sure to see the article when she returns tomorrow," she said quietly.

As Miss Trask led the way to the parked car, Honey and Trixie dropped back behind her. "I've got to talk to you," Trixie whispered, "but I *have* to do the chores that Moms didn't finish, or my folks won't let me out of the house for a month. Call me later this evening." Honey nodded, and they hurried to the car.

Miss Trask dropped Trixie off at Crabapple Farm. The governess had been very quiet since the revelation of the news article. *She's probably worried about Miss Darcy*, Trixie thought as she thanked her for the day.

Trixie trudged slowly up the driveway, lost in thought, her hands thrust in her coat pockets.

"Hey, Trixie!" Bobby shouted, seeming to have appeared out of nowhere.

Trixie looked up, startled. "Sorry, Bobby." She smiled when she saw his cheery, cold-reddened face. "My mind was a million miles away."

"Moms said you went to New York City. Is that a million miles away?" Bobby asked.

"No, honey." Trixie giggled at the question. "That's just an expression. It means that I was

159

thinking about something totally different from what I was doing."

"What were you doing?" the little boy asked. "And what's a 'spression?"

Trixie sighed. At some point in most conversations with Bobby, it was best to admit defeat.

"I'll try to explain it better later on," Trixie laughed. "Why don't you come inside for a while? I'll read you a story."

Bobby shook his head. "Nope. Can't. Reddy's getting his rest-up. I played and played with him all morning and after lunch. Then Moms said I should let him rest up for a while and I should go outside to play."

Trixie laughed again. "I'll bet you wore poor Reddy out with all that playing. Okay, I'll call you in later, after I finish my chores. Then I'll read a nice, quiet story to both you and Reddy."

"Okey-dokey," Bobby said happily, and he went back to the snowman he'd been building.

He's certainly in a good mood today. Trixie smiled to herself as she watched the little boy, bundled in heavy snow gear, clumsily attempt to pack more snow onto the lopsided figure he had created. *It must be because Reddy's home.*

Trixie was met by a barrage of teasing from

Mart as soon as she came in the back door.

"Ah, the lady of leisure has returned." He bowed low, doffing an imaginary hat. "While we slave away here on the old homestead, you're out enjoying the big, wide, wonderful world. Do tell, milady, how was the Big Apple today?"

"No more exciting than usual," Trixie replied casually, selecting an orange from the refrigerator. "Honey and I went to the museum while Miss Trask visited her sister, and then—" Trixie couldn't contain herself any longer, and without pausing for breath, she told Mart what the newspaper article said about Peter Ashbury.

"Whew!" Mart whistled. "I don't think it's humanly possible, using just the normal vocal apparatus, to articulate faster than you did just now. You might even qualify for the Guinness Book of World Records. Did you know, Trixie, that it takes the human ear at least one-fifteenth of a second to hear separate sounds?"

"Ma-art," Trixie said threateningly from between clenched teeth.

"Don't get me wrong." Mart held up his hands in a mock-defensive gesture. "I was just as impressed with the contents of what you said as with the speed at which you said it. I really think you've got something there," he said more seriously. "As wacky as you are sometimes, you *do* stumble onto some pretty interesting situations. But how do you put this together with the costumes and Miss Darcy?"

Trixie told him about having seen Miss Darcy removing "decorations" from one of the costumes. She also told him about her and Honey's sleuthing adventure that afternoon.

Mart frowned. "*That* was not very bright."

"But we didn't see the newspaper article until later," Trixie said defensively. "I only suspected that Ashbury was involved in something shady. I didn't expect to have my suspicions confirmed so soon!"

"You know, sometimes that sixth sense of yours is one heck of a criminal radar, Miss Sherlock. All suspicious characters within a fifty-mile radius, beware! Trixie Belden will find you out!" But he smiled at her with admiration. "Good work. Really, Trixie, I mean it. Now—"

He was interrupted by Helen Belden's frantic call from upstairs. "Will someone help me— please!"

Trixie and Mart both raced up the stairs, following the sound of their mother's voice. When they reached Bobby's room they tried to stifle their laughter when they saw their mother. She was down on her knees, with one finger stuck in the grating over a floor register. Reddy was at her side, with his foot wedged in beside her finger.

"Thank goodness you were inside the house!" Mrs. Belden cried when she saw them. "I was afraid everyone had gone outside."

"What happened?" Mart asked, surveying the situation.

"Ask for explanations later," Mrs. Belden groaned. "Right now, all I want to do is to get both Reddy and me out of this ridiculous predicament."

Trixie had gone to get a bottle of hand lotion. "Maybe if I squeeze some of this along Reddy's foot and on your finger, you can wiggle them out."

"Lubrication," Mart said. "Good idea."

"Mart," Trixie said, "we don't need a minute-by-minute report here; we need help! Try easing Reddy's foot out—slowly."

With a little maneuvering, Mrs. Belden and

Reddy were soon free. "Now. What happened?" Trixie asked.

Helen Belden laughed ruefully as she rubbed her sore finger. "I heard Reddy whining up here, so I came to see what was wrong. Apparently, he had been pawing at the grating with his foot and had gotten stuck. I tried to pull his foot out, but he had it wedged in there so tightly, it wouldn't move. So I very cleverly decided I would push it out from underneath with my finger—but then I got my finger stuck, too!"

"It's reassuring to know that sometimes even a mother gets into some pretty ridiculous situations," Mart laughed as the three of them walked down the stairs to the kitchen.

"Oh, my," Mrs. Belden said. "With all that excitement, I forgot to ask you: How was your trip to the city, Trixie?"

"Fine," Trixie said. "Honey and I poked around in the museum while Miss Trask visited her sister." She shot Mart a warning glance. Then she told her mother about the newspaper article.

"That's terrible!" Helen Belden exclaimed. "I feel sorry for Eileen Darcy—she seems like such a nice young woman. I wonder if she knows about it."

"Miss Trask doesn't think she does," Trixie answered.

"Well, maybe the young man is innocent," Mrs. Belden sighed. "Perhaps it was someone else in the jewelry store. He hasn't been proven guilty yet."

"True," Trixie agreed, "but—" She stopped, deciding it was best not to arouse her mother's suspicions by showing too much interest in Peter Ashbury.

"But what?" Mrs. Belden asked.

"Nothing." Trixie shrugged.

Mart had been quiet throughout the conversation, but now he intervened. "Hey, squaw," he teased, "there's about an inch of dust on everything in the den." He tossed her a dustcloth. "Flitting off to *museums* for the day doesn't get your chores done."

"Oh, yes," Mrs. Belden said. "That's one of things I didn't get done today. Would you please dust, Trixie?"

"Sure, Moms, and thanks again for giving me the day off."

"I'm afraid you won't have the evening off,"

her mother told her. "Your father and I are planning to go into town to see a movie and then have dinner. I'll have hamburgers and some other things ready for you here. I'm making plenty, so if you'd like to have Jim and Honey for dinner, it would be fine with me. You just have to be sure to keep Bobby entertained until his bedtime."

"No small feat, I might add," Mart said.

"That's for sure," Mrs. Belden sighed. "Between him and Reddy with that cast on, I'm surprised I got anything done today!"

"Thanks, Moms!" Trixie cried, giving her mother a quick hug. "It would be perfectly perfect to have Honey and Jim come for dinner. In fact, I'll call them right now."

"Dusting first," Mrs. Belden reminded her, "and then the phone call."

"Okay," Trixie agreed, and she headed for the den.

Mart followed her. "You were just about ready to open mouth and insert foot out there," he said in a whisper.

"I know," Trixie giggled. "Thanks for getting me off the hook by changing the subject. I almost said something about you-know-what."

She quickly dusted the room while Mart sprawled out, lounging lazily on the couch.

"You missed a spot near the lamp"—he pointed—"and near the bookcase. I hope you'll be able to pass the white-glove test," he teased.

"I think you've already passed the obnoxious test," Trixie sniffed.

"Peace, peace," Mart begged. "I'm really anxiously awaiting for you to finish so I can haul you upstairs and get the rest of the story about 'you-know-what,' " he whispered.

"You wouldn't think of helping me. . . ."

"Me?" Mart gasped. "Why, I—"

Trixie laughed at his shocked expression. "Yes, *you*! Hey," she said, suddenly changing the subject, "where are Brian and Dad? I haven't seen either one of them today."

"Dad took the car in for a tune-up, and Brian is over at the Wheelers' with Jim. They're helping Regan with the horses. In fact, I just came from there before you got home. Regan is pretty annoyed with us, you know. Under the threat of never being able to ride again, we all have to get over there and exercise the horses."

Trixie groaned. "I do feel guilty about that. It's just that it's so hard to do *everything*. We've

167

all been so busy lately. Regan is such a good sport about it, though—I don't want to get on his bad side."

"Well, I think Regan's good humor is fading fast, so I promised him we'd all be there bright and early tomorrow morning for a ride."

"Okay," Trixie agreed. She finished dusting the last piece of furniture and went into the kitchen to put away the cloth and polish.

Brian came in the back door carrying Bobby, who was covered with snow. "Look what I found in a snowdrift!" Brian laughed.

"Brian threw me in the snowdrift, then he founded me there." The little boy chortled happily as Brian set him down.

"Oh, no!" Mrs. Belden wailed. "My clean floor—now look at it!"

"Sorry, Moms," Brian apologized as he scooped Bobby up in his arms again. "I'll take him outside and de-snow him first."

When Brian and Bobby had returned and Trixie was helping her little brother out of his wet snowsuit, Brian leaned over and whispered in her ear. "Get on the hot line, kid. Your partner has something to tell you. She's already filled Jim and me in on the Ashbury news."

Trixie nodded, then nonchalantly announced that she was going to call and invite Jim and Honey to dinner.

"Tell them to come at about five o'clock," her mother called after her.

"Thanks, Moms, I will," Trixie responded as she dialed the Wheelers' number.

"What is it?" Trixie asked anxiously when Honey answered the phone.

"Trixie," Honey began excitedly, "Mother and Daddy came back early from Miami. Miss Trask showed them the newspaper article, and Mother does remember Mr. Ashbury, but she just never connected the name with Miss Darcy, and she'd never met him with her, so—"

"Yes, yes," Trixie interrupted impatiently.

"So," Honey went on, "she didn't realize it was the same person. Well, Mother said she thought he was married! In fact, she remembered distinctly that she once talked to him about his two children—"

"So that *wasn't* his sister!" Trixie interrupted. "Why, that. . . ."

"I know," Honey sighed. "Miss Trask feels just terrible about it—and, of course, I couldn't say that we saw him *and* his children *and* his wife today," she added in a whisper.

"I certainly hope not!" Trixie cried. "Honey, what about the jewelry your mother bought from Park Avenue Jewelers: Did Peter Ashbury sell it to her?"

"Yes," Honey answered. "Mother is going to arrange to remove it from the safe-deposit box the first thing Monday morning, and she and Daddy are taking it into New York City."

Trixie whistled. "It seems like *everyone* is getting involved in some way."

"It sure does," Honey agreed. "Oh, by the way, I told Jim and Brian—"

"I know," Trixie interrupted. "I told Mart, too. I just had to discuss it with someone. In fact, can you and Jim come here for dinner tonight? Moms and Dad are going out for the evening."

"We'd love to," Honey answered, "but Mother and Daddy just got home, and I don't know how they'd feel if Jim and I raced off to your house for dinner."

"Gleeps!" Trixie cried. "What a dope I am. Of course you should eat with them." She was well aware that Honey and Jim rarely saw their parents because they traveled so much. She knew that Honey sometimes envied the close relationship that the Beldens had with their parents, and so, whenever Honey's parents were home, she and Jim made a special effort to be with them.

"I'll see you and Jim first thing in the morning, anyway, and we'll talk then," Trixie assured her. "Mart informed me that Regan's going to be out for our blood if we don't exercise the horses."

"Yes," Honey said guiltily, "and you know what a temper he has!"

"Don't remind me," Trixie sighed. "Mart and Brian and I will be there. What about Di—is she coming, too?"

"No," Honey said. "I called and asked her, but she said she needed to stay home and practice her lines for the play."

"Trixie!" Helen Belden called.

"Oops, my dime must have run out," Trixie laughed. "Moms is calling me. I'll talk to you later." She said good-bye and hung up.

"Yes, Moms," Trixie answered, going into the kitchen.

"Your father and I are leaving now. Are Jim and Honey coming?"

Trixie explained why their friends wanted to stay home. Her mother nodded and said, "Well, you children have a nice evening."

As soon as Mr. and Mrs. Belden had left, Brian and Mart turned to Trixie.

"Okay, out with *everything*," Brian demanded, folding his arms and leaning against the kitchen counter. "Jim and I got a breathless account and only snatches of information from your sidekick. Now I want the whole story."

"And try not to exaggerate *too* much," Mart added.

"What does 'zaggerate mean, Mart?" Bobby asked.

"It's what your sister does about ninety-eight percent of the time," Mart chuckled.

Bobby looked at him quizzically. "I'll explain it while I give you a piggyback ride upstairs, Bobby," Brian said. "You and Reddy can play up there while we get dinner ready."

"Okey-dokey." Bobby smiled and hopped up on Brian's back.

"Small ears pick up a lot of big ideas," Trixie said to Mart after Brian and Bobby had left the room. "Sometimes I forget that he's around and that he listens to us!"

"And you know how well Bobby keeps a 'see-crud,' " Mart laughed.

"I know," Trixie sighed. "I'm afraid Bobby's love for secrets is only for the word itself."

Brian came back to the kitchen. "All right, time for the conference," he said. "Bobby is happily playing 'camping trip' with Reddy. He's made a tent with an old blanket."

Trixie related the whole story to her brothers. "And what do you make out of all this?" Brian asked when she'd finished.

"That's the trouble," Trixie sighed. "I definitely think those costumes and the catalog have something to do with it, but now we know that Peter Ashbury is a gemolgist and that he's married, and I can't figure out if Miss Darcy knows it, too, and is working with him, or—" Trixie stopped and her eyes widened. "That's it! He must be blackmailing her. Maybe he knows where her father is!"

"But the newspaper article said that Ashbury's been living in New York for the past six months," Brian pointed out.

"That's true," Trixie mused. "But those costumes are from England, and that's where Miss Darcy's father is. And come to think of it,"

Trixie said slowly, raising her eyes to look at her brothers, "that's where Miss Darcy was—up until *six months ago. . . .*"

At that moment, Bobby came running into the kitchen. "Hey, you guys, me and Reddy's tummies are grumbling."

"And what are they grumbling about?" Mart teased.

"They're hungry!" Bobby exclaimed. "And Reddy's tired of playing camping trip."

"Oh, no!" Trixie cried. "I completely forgot about the baked beans Moms left in the oven." She quickly grabbed two potholders.

"Hmmmm, *charred* beans is going to be more like it," Mart said, surveying the steaming dish Trixie had gingerly removed from the oven.

"Mart, why don't you try helping instead of criticizing," she snapped.

"Okay, okay!" he cried. "I'll fry the hamburgers. At least we'll have *something* to eat."

After dinner, Brian said that he and Mart would do the dishes—overriding Mart's howl of protest.

"I'll read to Bobby for a while," Trixie offered gratefully. She helped the little boy get ready for bed, then tucked him in. She began to feel very sleepy herself, though, as she read to him.

It's been a long day, Trixie sighed to herself. She glanced at Bobby. He was sound asleep, holding his teddy bear. Trixie kissed him lightly on the forehead and crept downstairs, where she found Mart and Brian watching television.

"Well, are you ready to tell us all your fantastic deductions, Miss Sherlock?" Mart asked.

Trixie yawned and stretched. "I'm too tired to tell deductions from reductions right now." She yawned again. "I'm going to hit the hay. See you bright and early for our ride."

It wasn't that she didn't want to tell Mart and Brian what she suspected, Trixie reasoned as she climbed the stairs. It was just that she wanted some time alone to really think things through, and she *was* exhausted. As she drifted off to sleep, though, questions kept running through her head. *What's the connection between the costumes and Peter Ashbury?* she wondered. *And where does Miss Darcy fit in all of it?*

Trixie awoke the next day to bright winter sunlight streaming through her windows. She got up and quickly pulled on a pair of dungarees and two heavy sweaters. *Got to bundle up for the ride*, she reminded herself.

. Mart and Brian were already in the kitchen eating breakfast when Trixie came downstairs.

"We were just about to come up and shag you out of bed, sleepyhead," Brian said.

The trio finished eating and donned heavy jackets. The morning was peacefully quiet as they walked over to Manor House. The only sound was the crunching of their footsteps through the crusty top layer of icy snow. Their boots sank into the six inches of soft powder beneath.

Jim and Honey were waiting for them at the stable. Regan had already saddled the horses. "I have to encourage you to ride these poor brutes as much as I can," he said gruffly.

"Gee, we're sorry, Regan, but it's hard to get away sometimes, with all the other things we have to do," Trixie explained.

Regan sighed, but his green eyes were twinkling. "Well, you'll only have yourselves to blame when spring rolls around and all we've got is a stableful of fat, lazy horses when you want to go riding every day."

Trixie swung up onto Lady, Honey took Strawberry, Jim rode Jupe, Brian chose Starlight, and Mart took Susie. They all started off at a slow gait.

The horses picked their way along the snow-covered path, their breath creating smokelike clouds in the cold air.

"They seem glad to be out," Honey said, gently stroking Strawberry's neck. "We have neglected them terribly."

They started toward the woods on the north side of Glen Road, when suddenly Trixie reined Lady to a halt. "Stop!" she hissed, and the others slowed their horses.

"What is it?" Jim whispered, but Trixie had already swung out of her saddle and dropped to the ground. She began running toward the woods.

"Hey!" Jim called after her. Then they heard a crackle of branches and the roaring of a car's engine. The three boys all swung down from their mounts and raced after Trixie.

Jewels and Jealousy · 10

WHAT WAS IT?" Honey demanded as the others returned to the clearing where she had stayed to watch the horses. Mart was limping, and blood dripped from a gash in his leg. "And what happened to *you*?" she cried.

"At least you had enough sense to stay behind and watch the horses," Jim said sheepishly. "We would have been in a fine mess with Regan if they had gotten away the way Trixie's 'spy' did."

Trixie broke in excitedly. "I *know* there was someone there! He was holding something in

178

front of his face—a camera or a pair of binoculars. When you called after me, Jim, he ran. You all heard the car start! I wish we could have gotten a good look at him, but we couldn't run through the snow fast enough. And then Mart tripped over a branch and went flying."

"Old eagle eyes here," Mart said, gingerly pulling back the tear in his jeans and examining the bloody gash.

Brian tied a clean handkerchief loosely around Mart's leg. "You'll live," he told his brother. Then he turned to Trixie. "Maybe that guy was just a friendly neighborhood bird watcher."

"Friendly neighborhood bird watchers don't take off like jackrabbits when they're spotted," Trixie retorted stubbornly. "That man was spying on us—I know it!"

"Maybe he was afraid of getting caught for trespassing on private property," Honey said.

"Ah, a sane, sensible explanation," Mart sighed.

Trixie glared. "You saw him run! You said you did! I don't think he was a bird watcher, but Honey may be right; he probably was afraid of getting caught, and not for trespassing, either. I have a sneaking suspicion that our sneaky spy was Peter Ashbury."

Brian's eyebrows shot up in surprise. "Trixie, I think you've got Ashbury on the brain. Anything the least bit mysterious that happens within the next week you'll blame on him. You may be right about his being a crook, but what in the world would he be doing here in the woods, on a cold Sunday morning?"

Trixie blushed. "I . . . I don't really know. But let's just ride down that road and take another look. Maybe we'll find a clue. How's your leg, Mart?"

"As Dr. Belden said, I'll survive, Trixie, but I don't see any point in looking again."

"If you don't want to come along, then don't," she said impatiently, and she turned Lady toward the old lane.

Mart sighed in resignation. "It *is* very tempting not to go with her," he said, as if Trixie weren't there. "If she's angry enough, she won't speak to us, which would be a nice reprieve. But then, again, she might stumble onto something interesting. . . ."

"Stumble!" Trixie cried indignantly. "It looks as though you're the only one who's stumbling today."

"Sure—on one of your wild-goose chases!"

Mart retorted. Trixie gave him a look that matched the morning's chill.

"Okay, that's enough!" Brian laughed. "I don't know about you two sometimes. Let's all go take another look at the tire tracks."

"What I don't understand," Honey said, "is how someone could drive on that old road with all this snow. It certainly hasn't been plowed or sanded all winter."

"Whoever it was wasn't driving a car," Jim explained. "We took a look at his tire tracks before, and he had either a small truck or a four-wheel drive vehicle. But I agree with Trixie: Let's go take another look. Maybe we *will* find a clue. He might have dropped his driver's license or something."

Trixie glanced sharply at Jim, but when she saw that he was half-teasing, she laughed good-naturedly. "I'm sorry I got so snappy. Sometimes I do act like a moron. It's just that I get so excited—"

"We know," Brian said, chuckling.

The Bob-Whites made their way over to the old back road and followed the fresh tracks out to the highway. They found nothing along the way that would identify the trespasser, and once on Glen Road, they couldn't distinguish his tire tracks among the slushy collection of hundreds of others.

Trixie was subdued as they finished their ride and slowly started back to the Wheeler estate.

Sensing her friend's mood, Honey drew Trixie aside as they were cleaning tack in the stable. "Don't worry, Trixie," she whispered. "We'll find out more tomorrow—I'm sure of it!"

Trixie grinned. "We sure will—or my name isn't Trixie Belden!"

The rest of the day was uneventful, and it seemed to drag on endlessly for Trixie. She had chores to do and homework to finish, and she helped to prepare Sunday dinner, but she couldn't wait for Monday morning to come. *I never thought I'd be excited about going to school.* She smiled to herself. *But I've got to see those costumes again*!

Monday morning finally came, and Trixie was the first one up. "My goodness!" her mother exclaimed when she saw her dressed and ready for school. "Did you get up before the sun this morning?"

"Almost," Trixie laughed. "I woke up early

and couldn't get back to sleep."

Trixie had almost finished her breakfast by the time the rest of the family sat down at the table. Brian and Mart grumbled as their sister hurried them through their meal, into their coats, and out to the bus stop. As they waited, Trixie anxiously shifted her books from one arm to the other. "Of all mornings for that bus to be late!" she wailed.

"Patience, Beatrix," Mart said, glancing at his watch. "The bus isn't late; we're early. You'll get to school on time."

"Obviously it's not school she's worried about," Brian said. "What is it, Trix—some quick sleuthing before the first bell?"

"I've got a plan that I'm dying to put into action," she answered mysteriously.

"Are you going to let us in on it, or do you plan to wait until the last minute to call for our expert assistance?" Mart probed.

"You'll have to wait," Trixie sniffed as the bus finally arrived and they boarded.

But there was no time to set the wheels of her plan in motion, because the bus arrived at school just in time for her first class.

"How come," Trixie wailed as she and Honey

hurried to their lockers, "when I actually plan something, get up early, and for once in my life am *completely* organized, something happens to ruin the whole thing?"

Trixie slid into her seat as the general school announcements were being made over the PA system. At the end, there was a special announcement from the principal.

"Students," he began in a very stern voice, "as those of you who are involved with the freshman class play know, several Shakespearean costumes were very graciously lent to us by a friend of Miss Darcy's. One of those costumes, a velvet gown, has disappeared. Any student who has any information concerning the whereabouts of this costume, please come forward at once and report either to Miss Darcy or to me. The costume was last seen by Miss Darcy on Friday evening after school."

Trixie gasped and sat bolt upright in her seat. *Now what?* she wondered. *Can it be Peter Ashbury again? Oh, I can't wait until rehearsal!* But she didn't have to wait that long. Half an hour after the first announcement, the PA system clicked on again.

"Trixie Belden and Diana Lynch," a voice

commanded, "please report to Miss Darcy's office immediately." Trixie stood up at once, and her science teacher, Mr Morrison, nodded. She left the classroom, and as she hurried toward the drama club office, she met Di in the hallway.

"Do you think it has something to do with the missing costume?" Di whispered nervously.

"I certainly hope so!" Trixie answered.

"My goodness, why?" Di asked, her face clouding with concern and confusion.

"Oh, Di," Trixie said quickly, seeing the perplexed look on her friend's pretty face. "I'm sorry. We've really kept you in the dark about this whole thing. You've been so busy with the play. Don't worry," she reassured her as they neared Miss Darcy's office. "Leave this to me, and I'll explain everything later."

Eileen Darcy was waiting for them. She had the haggard, dark-eyed look of someone who had not slept well for several days.

"Now, girls," she began calmly, "this is a very serious matter indeed, and I expect that you will be honest with me. We have reason to believe that you had something to do with the disappearance of the costume, and—"

"What?" Trixie cried, wide-eyed with disbelief. "Why—Who—" she stammered as her cheeks flushed crimson. Di began biting her nails nervously.

"Please, Trixie, let me finish!" Miss Darcy said sharply. She drew a deep breath and went on more calmly. "Now, you were here on Friday after school. When I returned to my office after walking you to the front entrance, the costume I had been . . . working on was gone."

"But why do you suspect us?" Trixie cried. "If I was with you and Di was out waiting in the car—"

"That is true," Miss Darcy answered. "However, someone reported that you and—"

"Why would we want the costume?" Di interrupted. "Really, Miss Darcy, I—we had nothing to do with it!"

"Yes," Trixie demanded angrily. "Why would we take it? And who said that we did? What proof do they have?"

"I—I'm sorry. I am not permitted to say," Miss Darcy answered. Then suddenly she buried her face in her hands, and her body shook with sobs.

"Miss Darcy?" Trixie ventured quietly. "I

know those costumes are very important to you—"

"You—you couldn't possibly know how important." The drama teacher squared her shoulders and again drew a deep breath, trying to regain her composure.

Trixie looked directly at Miss Darcy. "If you'll give me until tomorrow morning, I promise I'll find that costume for you."

Eileen Darcy looked away from Trixie's steady gaze. "I don't know what to do anymore," she said despairingly. "If you could help, I wouldn't know how to thank you. That costume is very important to my—my friend in England."

"Please, Miss Darcy," Trixie pleaded, "let me try."

"Very well," she answered more hopefully. "I didn't really believe you two had taken the gown." She smiled weakly. "Run along, now. I'll see you both in class. And Trixie, the moment you—"

"I know," Trixie said as they left the office. "Don't worry."

Trixie could hardly contain her excitement. "How can I possibly go back and sit through two more classes before I—" She stopped, seeing the bewildered look on Di's face. "Oh, Di!" she cried. "There's so much I have to explain!" Trixie quickly gave her friend a summary of what had happened so far. Di listened quietly, her eyes growing bigger as Trixie related each episode.

"Sometimes I think I must be as blind as a bat," Di sighed. "All of this was going on right under my nose, and I didn't suspect a thing! Who do you think told Miss Darcy that we took the costume?"

"Why, Peter Ashbury, of course."

"But, Trixie," Di said, thinking hard, "how could he have told Miss Darcy, unless he was here this morning between the first announcement and the one asking for us? I suppose he could have called her, but don't you think it was probably someone in school?"

"Di! You're absolutely right!" Trixie cried, giving her friend a quick hug. "What an idiot I am! Mart was right when he said that I have a one-track mind sometimes."

Di looked confused again. "Don't you see?" Trixie explained. "It must have been Jane Morgan who told Miss Darcy that we took the costume—" She was interrupted by the sound of the second-hour bell. Students began pouring out of classrooms, filling the hallway. "I'll tell you the rest later," Trixie promised as she and Di parted and hurried to their classes.

The next two hours were torture for Trixie, but finally they were over, and she hurried to the auditorium. She stationed herself at the entrance to the wardrobe room and waited for Jane Morgan.

"Jane." Trixie stopped her in the hallway. "Could I talk to you for a minute?"

"About what?" Jane snapped.

"About the velvet gown," Trixie answered evenly, reminding herself to keep calm.

Jane shrugged. "What about it?"

"You know what I mean. You have it!"

"How dare you accuse me—"

"The same way you accused me," Trixie interrupted coldly.

Jane looked away and didn't answer. Trixie went on, "Listen, I don't care about you, and you obviously don't like me, either, but that costume is more important than you think. It could really be a matter of life or death for Miss Darcy!"

Jane eyed her suspiciously. "I always knew you were nosy and got involved where you didn't belong, Trixie Belden, but I didn't know you were so melodramatic."

Trixie was furious. "*You're* the actress!" she snapped.

Jane turned on her heel and stalked into the wardrobe room, slamming the door behind her. Trixie stood in the narrow corridor, angrily clenching and unclenching her fists. *I'll find that costume yet!* she vowed to herself.

All through drama class, Trixie was seething, and at the lunch table, her anger finally erupted. Sputtering with indignation, she related the morning's events to the rest of the Bob-Whites.

Jim whistled when she had finished. "It looks as if you have an honest-to-goodness mystery here now."

"But, Trixie," Honey asked, "why do you suspect Jane, and not Peter Ashbury, of taking the costume?"

"He could have taken it," Trixie admitted. "I think they both want it, but for different reasons. I have a feeling that Jane wanted to get Di in trouble so that she would be kicked out of the play."

"Of course!" Di cried. "You are so smart sometimes!"

"Not always," Trixie laughed dryly. "In fact, Di, you're the one who made me suspect Jane instead of Ashbury. Now I've got to figure out how to get her to admit it. Do you think I could get a search warrant?"

"How about a polygraph?" Mart suggested teasingly.

"A polly what?" Di asked.

"A lie detector," Mart explained.

Trixie jumped up. "That's it!" she cried, gathering up her books.

"You're going to give Jane a lie-detector test?" Brian asked laughingly.

"No, but I do have an idea that I think will make Jane more than happy to tell me everything she knows about that costume."

Trixie got up and quickly scanned the lunchroom, searching for Jane and her friends. She finally spotted Patty Morris at a table on the far side of the room. She strolled over casually.

"Patty," Trixie asked, "do you know where Jane is?"

"She went home." Patty shrugged. "She said she felt as if she was getting the flu."

I'll bet she did! Trixie thought. "Okay, thanks," she said nonchalantly.

"Well?" Honey asked eagerly when Trixie returned.

"Jane went home sick," she explained. "I think we should go and visit her after school, Honey, don't you? She only lives a few blocks from here. We'll just drop by to see how she's feeling." She grinned at Honey mischievously. "Brian, will you please tell Moms that Honey and I had to stay late tonight and that we'll take a cab home?"

"I don't know about this, Trixie," Jim said doubtfully. "Maybe one of us should go with you."

"Nonsense!" Trixie cried. "*I* have everything under control."

Trixie spent the rest of the afternoon planning exactly what she was going to say to Jane, but it turned out to be unnecessary. Jane was waiting for her when she and Honey got out of their last class.

"Jane!" Trixie exclaimed in surprise. "I thought you went home."

"I did," the girl said nervously, "but I had to talk to you."

"Why don't we get away from this crowd?" Trixie suggested. The three girls turned down a side corridor and found an empty bench to sit on.

"Actually, I am kind of scared," Jane said nervously. "I supposedly went home sick today. If any of my teachers should see me—"

"Wasn't your mother suspicious when you wanted to come back to school at three o'clock?" Honey asked.

"My mom isn't home during the day," Jane explained. "She works. I just spent the afternoon alone—thinking." Trixie and Honey waited for her to go on. "You'll miss your bus if I don't hurry up and tell you," she said in a distracted way.

"Don't worry about that, Jane. We'll get home later. Now, what is it?" Trixie asked impatiently.

"I-It's very hard for me to admit," Jane began hesitantly, lowering her eyes. "You see, I didn't mean to keep the dress. I—I just . . . borrowed it for a while."

"Where is it?" Trixie asked.

"It's at home, in my closet," Jane said, her eyes filling with tears. "I don't know what to do. I suppose I should go tell Miss Darcy.''

"No," Trixie said quickly. "Come on, let's go get the dress, and then we'll come back and tell her."

"Trixie!" Honey cried. "You know—"

"I *do* know," Trixie said, "finally! But I want to make sure. Come on, let's go!"

As the three girls walked the five blocks to the Morgan house, Jane desperately tried to explain. "You see, I wanted to play the part of Juliet so much, and Di looked so beautiful in that costume, I just couldn't stand it anymore. I heard you tell my uncle when you came to pick up Reddy on Friday that you were going back to school, and I thought. . . .''

"If you took the dress and blamed it on us, Di would be out of the play," Trixie finished for her.

"That's right." Jane nodded sadly. "I'm so sorry. I really am ashamed of myself.''

You should be, Trixie thought, but she held her tongue. "Actually, that isn't important now. You can apologize to Miss Darcy—and to Di—later. Right now, we've got to get that costume."

The three girls arrived at the Morgan house

and quickly got the velvet gown from Jane's closet.

"See—here it is, safe and sound," Jane sighed.

"Now we've got to get right back to Miss Darcy's office," Trixie urged.

"I hope you know what you're doing," Honey said uncertainly.

"Of course I do," Trixie answered. "Now, let's hurry." Trixie carried the dress as they raced back to school.

"I'm sorry about this whole thing," Jane apologized again as she knocked on Miss Darcy's office door. "I guess I got carried away with my own jealousy. I really didn't mean to hurt anyone or get you in trouble."

"We know," Honey said sympathetically.

"Miss Darcy must not be here. See if the door is unlocked," Trixie said impatiently.

Jane turned the knob. "It's open, but I don't think we should—"

"Gleeps! You're as bad as Honey is sometimes!" Trixie wailed. She pushed past Jane into the office. "I think Miss Darcy is in trouble. We've got to help her."

Trixie laid the costume on a chair, and Jane and Honey glanced nervously around the room.

195

"The catalog first," Trixie said, her eyes searching the office. "Here it is!" she cried excitedly as she pounced on the catalog. She quickly turned the pages until she found the illustration of the velvet gown. "Now, there's got to be something about this. . . ." she mused.

"I feel funny being here," Jane said. "I'm in enough trouble already."

"So do I," Honey shuddered. "It's as if we're on the verge of getting caught for something that we're not supposed to be doing, which we aren't supposed to be . . . I mean, we *aren't* supposed to be in here!"

"Honey, puh-leeze!" Trixie begged. "Whenever you start talking like that, I know you're nervous. Besides, I'm trying to concentrate on— Omigosh! Look at this!" Honey and Jane hurried to her side.

"See?" Trixie said, almost squealing, and pointing to the illustration of the velvet gown. "This picture is different. All the others are plain black and white, but this one's colored in. Quick, hand me the dress. So *that's* what Miss Darcy was 'fixing!' " Trixie cried as she spread the dress out on the desk and examined it carefully.

Both Jane and Honey looked puzzled. Trixie continued to explain. "See, some of the costume decorations in the picture are colored in blue pencil. Now, look at the dress. Miss Darcy has removed some of the decorations already, but there are a lot more, according to this picture, that she obviously didn't have time to cut off before Jane took the dress."

Honey gasped. "Those aren't just paste decorations, then. They're—"

"Real jewels," Trixie affirmed grimly.

Jane turned pale. "You mean—" Trixie nodded. "I think I'm going to faint," Jane said.

"Oh, for goodness sake, don't do that," Trixie said impatiently. "We need your help."

"Mine?" Jane squeaked.

"Yes." Trixie's tone was firm. "I want you to call Miss Darcy at home right now and admit to taking the costume. Ask her to come here immediately, and then—"

"But, Trixie," Jane interrupted, "I don't know if I can do it!"

"Of course you can. You were going to have to tell her, anyway," Trixie said decisively. She picked up the catalog once more, and as she did an envelope slipped out and drifted to the floor.

Trixie picked it up quickly. It was unsealed, and the contents spilled out.

"Here's that safe-deposit receipt and the pictures of the costumes again. But what's this?" She unfolded a tissue-thin piece of paper, then gasped as she read it. "Listen!" she cried:

"Miss Darcy: Within the next several days, you will be receiving a catalog from the Shakespearean Costume Company of London. A certain costume will be marked with light blue shading, indicating the placement of valuable gems. Several days after you receive the catalog, the costumes will arrive. You are to remove the gems, as indicated in the catalog, and store them in a safe-deposit box that has been registered in your name at the First National Bank of Sleepyside, New York. You will be contacted and instructed as to where the jewels are to be delivered. If you notify the police or anyone else about this matter, you will never see your father again. Beware. You are being watched carefully."

Jane leaned heavily against the wall. "You were right, then," she said shakily. "I didn't quite believe that those jewels were real. It's just so hard to imagine—I feel like I'm in a movie or something!"

"You're not used to Trixie," Honey said,

"although even *that* isn't much help now. I'm shocked, too."

"This must be the letter that Miss Darcy said she received the night of the accident with Reddy," Trixie mused, "but it certainly isn't from a 'friend.'" She added slowly, "No wonder she was so upset! And you know, I think the person who intends to pick up those jewels is none other than our old friend Peter Ashbury."

Trixie picked up the phone and dialed directory assistance. "We've got to let her know that we've got the dress, before Ashbury finds out it was missing, or else her father—" She broke off abruptly. "The number for Eileen Darcy in Sleepyside, please. . . . Thank you," she said, writing hurriedly. She broke the connection, then dialed Miss Darcy's number.

"There's no answer!" Trixie wailed, dropping the receiver back into its cradle. "I wonder if— We'd better call for a cab right away." She picked up the phone again.

"I think we should call the police," Jane said nervously. "If there are *real* jewels involved and a *real* kidnapping. . . ."

"It's real enough, all right," Trixie said, "but we're not going to call the police. Not yet,

199

anyway. We've got to get to your house, Honey."

"My house? Why?"

"Whom do you think Miss Darcy would turn to if she were in trouble—especially now, when the only thing that can save her father has been stolen?"

"Miss Trask!" Honey cried. "Of course! You are so smart, Trixie."

"I'm afraid I'm not smart enough soon enough, sometimes," she groaned as she dialed the cab service.

The door of the office flew open. "Your cab is already here," Peter Ashbury snarled. Honey and Jane whirled around. Trixie gulped as her eyes fell on the gun in his hand.

"I know it's impolite to eavesdrop," he said, "but I couldn't help overhearing your interesting conversation. So you think you've got the whole thing figured out, do you? Come on, you little snoops," he said harshly, motioning toward the door. "I'll be glad to give you a lift. After all, I do owe you a favor. You found the dress, and you're leading me right to Eileen Darcy."

The three girls stood paralyzed with fear.

"Come on!" he snapped again, grabbing the catalog and envelope from Trixie's hands. "That stupid woman—leaving this stuff around for anyone to find!"

He picked up the dress and folded it over the gun. "Now, move! I've got the car parked in the back lot. And don't try anything tricky, or you'll all be sorry," he threatened. They filed out of the office and walked slowly down the corridor.

The Final Curtain · 11

TRIXIE SILENTLY PRAYED that someone would still be in one of the classrooms, or the janitor would be working, or that Miss Darcy would suddenly return—anything to stop them before they left the building.

I don't dare run or scream, she thought desperately. *I don't even know if I could muster the strength to whimper right now!*

She felt as if she were in a bad dream, and that if only she could concentrate hard enough, she would wake up and it would all be over. She glanced back at Peter Ashbury.

"I meant what I said," he whispered hoarse-ly. "Not one sound."

Trixie nodded. *Poor Jane and Honey*, she commiserated silently. *If I'm petrified, I can't imagine what they feel like!*

They left the school building by the rear en-trance, and Ashbury herded the three girls across the parking lot to a jeeplike vehicle.

"You two get in the back," he growled, wav-ing the gun at Honey and Jane. "And you, Sherlock—in front with me."

Trixie looked at the other two girls. Their faces were white with fear. *I've got to do some-thing!* she thought frantically as she climbed in-to the front seat. *Maybe I can jump from the car if he isn't going too fast—but then where would I be? And that would mean leaving Honey and Jane alone. Maybe I could get the gun from him.* But she quickly dismissed that idea, know-ing she'd never be able to fire it, even if she could get it.

Ashbury headed out of town, taking Glen Road toward the Wheeler estate.

"So you know where Manor House is," Trixie said, as calmly as she could. "Have you been there before?"

Ashbury laughed. "Yes. I did some exploring yesterday. Nice little setup Matthew Wheeler has there. I would have hung around to say hello to you, but I was in a hurry."

"So that *was* you in the woods yesterday," Trixie cried. "I thought—"

"You'd be wise to keep your thoughts to yourself, Little Miss Detective. All I want is the jewels that have already been removed from the costume, and then I'll disappear—just like magic—never to be seen again."

"But—" Trixie began.

"And no more questions from you," he snapped. "I don't intend to be interrogated by a high school kid."

As they rounded a curve in the road, Trixie glanced in the rearview mirror attached to the outside of her door. She smiled faintly and gave a secret sigh of relief, for close behind was the Bob-White station wagon. *They must have come back to school to pick us up*, she thought, her heart beginning to beat faster. *They must have seen us; they had to*!

Trixie glanced at Peter Ashbury. The gun lay in his lap and he had one hand covering it protectively. *Don't let him notice that they're following us!* she prayed silently.

Ashbury turned into the long drive, dousing his headlights as they approached the Wheeler mansion. Miss Darcy's car was parked near the back entrance

"Okay, kids, out!" he ordered. "You go in first." He shoved Honey toward the front door.

"Is that you, Honey?" Miss Trask called from the living room as Ashbury came in behind the girls and closed the door.

"Y-Yes," Honey answered shakily.

"Let's all go in and join their little discussion," Ashbury whispered. The three girls obediently headed toward the parlor.

Eileen Darcy gave a startled cry as Ashbury walked into the room, the black gun gleaming ominously in his hand.

"What's going on?" Miss Trask demanded coldly.

"It isn't a cocktail party," Ashbury snarled. "I hadn't counted on a mess like this, but all kinds of little surprises creep up, even in the best of plans. Or should I say that little creeps can be a big surprise?" He glared evilly at Trixie.

"Peter!" Miss Darcy cried. "Please don't hurt them. I was the one—"

"You certainly were," he snarled. "Now, where are the jewels you've already taken off the costume?"

"They're still in the safe-deposit box. I— How is my father? Is he all right? Is he—"

"Alive?" Ashbury supplied for her. "Oh, he's alive—for now. All I want are those gems. Your little friends graciously supplied me with the gown, but I'm afraid I wouldn't have a matched set if I didn't get the rest of the jewels."

"Peter," Eileen Darcy said bitterly, "I don't understand this elaborate plan. Why didn't you just have your 'friends' in England—whoever they are—send the gems directly to you?"

"One newspaper article will answer that question," Trixie said.

Ashbury laughed dryly. "So you read the newspaper, too."

Eileen Darcy looked from Trixie to Miss Trask. The older woman nodded sadly.

Trixie eyed Ashbury thoughtfully. "Apparently," she mused, "there's more than just the New York jewel theft involved here. He must have pulled the same thing in England, and maybe the police started getting too close over there. But he couldn't have his cohorts send the loot directly to him because, by that time, things were getting pretty hot over here, too. . . .''

"That's enough!" Ashbury shouted. He turned on Miss Darcy. "All you had to do was remove the stones and put them in the bank. An easy enough job in exchange for your father's life, don't you think? But then this kid had to go and see the catalog, and that other one had to take those pictures—"

"So you did take the film from Bill Morgan's camera," Trixie said, but Ashbury ignored her.

"All this chitchat is wasting valuable time. Come on, Eileen." Ashbury grabbed her roughly by the arm. "We've got a little bank business to do in town, and we'd better hurry. The bank is open only for another half hour." He backed out of the room, using Miss Darcy as a shield. "If any of you should decide to call the police anytime within the next two hours, I'm afraid Mr. Darcy won't be found in very good health. I'll okay his release when I'm safely out of the country, but not a second before."

"Wait!" Trixie cried, stalling for time, hoping that her brothers and Jim would arrive soon with the police. "Why don't you take me along,

207

too? Who's going to be your hostage while Miss Darcy's in the bank?"

"No, Trixie!" Eileen Darcy cried.

"Not a bad idea, kid," Ashbury said. "A little extra insurance never hurt. Come on, then. Let's go. Remember," he called back to Honey, Jane, and Miss Trask. "Two hours."

Trixie felt a strange calmness settle over her as she walked through the kitchen with Miss Darcy beside her and Peter Ashbury behind her. *I wonder why I'm not frightened?* she thought curiously.

As she stepped out the back door into the frosty winter dusk, Trixie caught the flicker of a shadow at the corner of the house. "Run!" she hissed to Miss Darcy, and they took off through the snow. Immediately Brian, Mart, Jim, and Regan closed in on Ashbury. They quickly overpowered him, and Regan knocked the gun from Ashbury's hand.

"Okay, boys, hold him tight until the nice policemen get here." Regan smirked as he picked up the revolver.

Just then they heard the welcome wail of a siren.

"Right on cue," Mart said.

Trixie felt as if her whole body had been reduced to a jellied mass. "I have never been so happy to see all of you in my life!" she cried.

Miss Trask, Honey, and Jane appeared at the back door. "Thank goodness you're all safe!" Miss Trask sighed.

Peter Ashbury stood silent, glowering at all of them as two police cars pulled up into the driveway.

Sergeant Molinson stepped out of the lead car. "I should have known." He shook his head. "Another Belden case."

"But, Sergeant Molinson—" Trixie began. Accustomed to his scolding about her sleuthing adventures, she was always quick to defend herself and her methods.

"First, the prisoner," Molinson interrupted, stopping her with a don't-push-me-too-far look. Trixie nodded as the sergeant snapped a pair of handcuffs on Ashbury and informed him of his rights.

"Now," the policeman continued, turning to Miss Darcy, "I presume you are Eileen Darcy." The young drama teacher nodded. "You'll be happy to know that your father is alive and well. About half an hour ago, we received a call from the British Embassy. Apparently, Scotland Yard has been working on a case involving a ring of jewel smugglers. They finally broke the ring this afternoon and arrested two suspects—friends of Ashbury's, here. Finding your father was a bonus. Ashbury's partners obligingly informed the detectives of Mr. Darcy's whereabouts. We were asked to contact you. Your father is in a London hospital for a few days' rest. We have information about where you may reach him."

"Thank God," Miss Darcy sobbed. Miss Trask stepped forward quietly and put her arms around the young woman.

"Now, Trixie." Molinson turned a stern eye on her. "With all this international espionage, how did *you* get involved? I'm not quite sure I want to know, but some kind of morbid curiosity compels me to ask."

"It's a little chilly out here," Miss Trask broke in smoothly. "Why don't we all go inside and have a cup of coffee? I still feel a little weak-kneed from this whole experience. We can listen to Trixie's story inside."

"Good idea," Molinson said. "You go in. There are some officers coming up from New

York City, and they should be here soon. We contacted them, and they offered to come right out and pick up Ashbury. They're very interested in what he has to say."

The rest of the group filed into the Wheelers' living room. Miss Darcy sat down and sighed deeply. "I don't even know where to begin!" she said softly. "I'm so happy that my father is safe, and Trixie, I don't know how to begin to thank you."

"Well, I know where *Trixie* can begin," Sergeant Molinson said as he entered the room and took a seat. "She can begin her story at the beginning."

Trixie told them the whole story, with additions from Honey and Jane about the evening's encounter with Ashbury.

"Trixie was wonderful!" Jane said with admiration. "She had the whole thing figured out, and—"

Trixie blushed. "Everything was in the letter, Jane," she said, embarrassed. "I didn't really—"

"Hey, how about a little praise and adulation for the last-minute rescuers?" Mart asked.

"You three and Regan were terrific," Trixie said quickly. "Really! When we started to run, I was absolutely petrified, even though I knew you were there, around the corner."

"It must have been that sixth sense of yours," Jim chuckled.

"Well, no," Trixie admitted. "First I saw you in the rearview mirror of Ashbury's car, following us in the station wagon."

"You did?" Honey cried. "No wonder you were so calm—or acted like it, anyway. Jane and I were so scared." She shuddered. "I thought I would faint dead away with fear."

"I figured they must have come back to school to pick us up," Trixie explained, "and saw us get into Ashbury's car."

"Exactly," Brian agreed. "We thought something was fishy, so we decided to follow you. We parked at the end of the drive and walked the rest of the way. Then Jim did a quick spying job through the living room windows, and when he saw Ashbury with the gun, we went to Regan's apartment over the garage and telephoned the police—and the rest is history!"

Sergeant Molinson began grumbling about their methods and reminding them that a phone call to him sooner would have made things a lot easier on everyone.

"But a lot less exciting," Trixie murmured.

"That kind of excitement," Miss Trask said decisively, "we can live without!" Everyone laughed.

Jane Morgan humbly apologized to Miss Darcy for taking the costume. "I'll tell Di how sorry I am, too," she added. "And I want to tell all of you that I think you're terrific. I used to think—well, that doesn't really matter anymore, because I can see how wrong I was. You really are a great detective, Trixie. Even though I was scared to death tonight, detective work *is* exciting. I wonder if—"

"Oh, no!" Sergeant Molinson groaned and threw up his hands. "One Trixie Belden around here is enough!"

"Hear! Hear!" Mart cried enthusiastically.

"Yes, but—" Jane continued. "How do you *find* a mystery?"

"I don't think you quite understand yet, Jane," Brian explained, chuckling. "Mysteries seem to find Trixie!" Everyone joined in the laughter.

"That's true," Trixie said, her blue eyes sparkling, "and I hope there's another one looking for me right now!"

213

YOU WILL ENJOY

THE TRIXIE BELDEN SERIES

34 Exciting Titles

TRIXIE BELDEN MYSTERY-QUIZ BOOKS

2 Fun-Filled Volumes

THE MEG MYSTERIES

6 Baffling Adventures

ALSO AVAILABLE

Algonquin
Alice in Wonderland
A Batch of the Best
More of the Best
Still More of the Best
Black Beauty
The Call of the Wild
Dr. Jekyll and Mr. Hyde
Frankenstein
Golden Prize
Gypsy from Nowhere
Gypsy and Nimblefoot
Gypsy and the Moonstone Stallion
Lassie—Lost in the Snow
Lassie—The Mystery of Bristlecone Pine
Lassie—The Secret of the Smelters' Cave
Lassie—Trouble at Panter's Lake
Match Point
Seven Great Detective Stories
Sherlock Holmes
Shudders
Tales of Time and Space
Tee-Bo and the Persnickety Prowler
Tee-Bo in the Great Hort Hunt
That's Our Cleo
The War of the Worlds
The Wonderful Wizard of Oz